Books by Randolph Lalonde

THE CHAOS CORE SERIES
Trapped
Cool Pursuit

THE SPINWARD FRINGE SERIES
Spinward Fringe Broadcast 0: Origins
Spinward Fringe Broadcast 1 and 2: Resurrection and
Awakening
Spinward Fringe Broadcast 3: Triton
Spinward Fringe Broadcast 4: Frontline
Spinward Fringe Broadcast 5: Fracture
Spinward Fringe Broadcast 6: Fragments
The Expendable Few: A Spinward Fringe Novel
Spinward Fringe Broadcast 7: Framework
Spinward Fringe Broadcast 8: Renegades
Spinward Fringe Broadcast 9: Warpath
Spinward Fringe Broadcast 10: Freeground

Brightwill

Dark Arts

For more information please visit:
www.RandolphLalonde.com

TRAPPED

CHAOS CORE BOOK 1

Randolph Lalonde

EBook ISBN: 978-1-9881750-4-1

Year 998.4 United Core Authority Calendar
The beginning of the Basic Era

Humanity is slowly recovering from a galactic holocaust. After a virus that turned artificial intelligences against them ravaged the population and reduced centuries old systems of law and order to mere memory, the once civilized core worlds have become mostly lawless territory. Mostly.

The United Core Authority discovered a tool, a new virus they began using to prevent artificial intelligences from communicating with other computer systems digitally, reducing their effectiveness and turning the tide of the war. Along with a campaign to neutralize advanced technology that is not under control, they have managed to quiet the open war that threatened to end humanity in a growing group of solar systems.

New wars begin, some driven by artificial intelligences who have become trapped in single metal chassis, others conducted by humans with grand ideas and too much hardware. Any spacer will tell you that the conflict map changes daily, and while that provides opportunity for some, it is also a constant source of danger.

Slavery is the fastest growing industry now that mankind has lost trust in intelligent machines. People of all ages run the risk of being captured and sold if they are caught alone on the streets by certain gangs, governments or corporations. The drive to reclaim technology that was once used to create enhanced and custom humans is on. There are examples of this golden age of human production from before the Holocaust, when artificial intelligences turned on their masters. They were made from entirely synthetic reproductive materials, customized to have restricted life spans and unrestricted potential. They are called dolls. Some of them were able to escape during the Holocaust, others remain in service to their masters, but they are all highly sought after since the laboratories and other facilities responsible for their creation are surrounded by armies led by artificial intelligences that will do anything to prevent humanity from getting their hands on the tools for progress in the Geist System.

Through this, the elements of humanity that were already used to hiding – criminals and the ultra-wealthy – have thrived in their own ways. The difference between the two have become only skin deep, and they control the spaces where humanity tries to thrive. Both sides are ruthless in their quest to be in power when order is restored, while the United Core Authority operates as a military dictatorship on the few worlds they can afford to police regularly.

Near one of those systems, a spacer named Aspen Dunewell enjoys her leave from the Cool Angel, a small armed freighter that does whatever work the Captain can find for her crew. Aspen is completely unaware that she's about to be drawn into the middle of humanity's next struggle in the Core Worlds.

01

Dancing. Aspen Dunewell loved everything about dancing. The aggressive punch and pound of the music set her bouncing and swaying with her eyes closed. They were the Pip Divers, a Joy Metal band with two females and one male singer, all of whom had mastered ancient instruments using strings and picks. She loved the distortion, the utter aggression of it, and the powerful beat provided by a woman who played old style drums behind everyone else. Aspen would go see her later, at least to tell her that she made her feel like dancing for the first time in a long time.

The crowd around her was a crew she'd come to know, they protected their own, leaving her free to 'look good and groove.' It was a term her Lieutenant, Sun, used when they were getting ready for leave that afternoon. The lower and middle ranks had become like her family, a good thing, since space on the Cool Angel was tight.

The cream coloured dress Aspen borrowed from Sun flowed and swayed loosely while keeping her covered. The top half was a single loose circle of cloth that drooped from her neck, leaving her back bare. The bottom half was a short skirt that teased at showing what was underneath but would not creep up or down thanks to programmable surface cloth, so she could comfortably sway, grind and bump as much as she wanted. She hadn't worn anything that felt so good in a year.

Her hip bumped against someone, and she half-turned her head to see Boro, a crewman she'd been talking to and flirting with for two months. They'd had what she liked to call 'a date of opportunity' more than once, talking late into the evening in the mess hall after she'd finished helping Cookie clean up. He was a little thick in the middle, allergic to body shaping meds – not that he could have afforded them – and she was sure he liked her too much for some easy going fun, but she fancied him anyway, so he earned a wink instead of a sneer on most days. He smiled and danced behind her as she ground to the beat a little. He kissed her on the neck, put a hand on her bare waist. Boro, a fabricator by trade who could make any complicated part with the right materials, had a surprisingly warm, nice touch as his fingers splayed out under her top, and he teased her neck with light kisses.

Sun, the raven-haired Lieutenant she provided support for – that was Aspen's only job – was dancing in front of her. She was in a dress of a similar style, only her slimmer figure was tightly wrapped instead of loosely covered, and the fabric was so black it seemed to drink the light in. The smile across her glossy black lips and approving nod told Aspen that she'd have some personal time that night. Aspen smiled back as Boro kissed her lightly under her earlobe, sending tingles through her. She'd never seen Boro pair up with anyone in the year she'd served aboard the Cool Angel, he most likely had a lot of energy to spend. She slid her hand atop his and leaned her head back; "Take it slow," she said over the music. Boro's head came up so his lips were next to hers. "Sorry," he said.

"We have all night," she said and kissed him, tasting the strong fermented cocktail he'd had, a very obvious mood enhancer she recognized right away called Valentia. Aspen ground against him several times, she wanted him to feel encouraged. With what she loaded onto the station credit chit she had tucked into her skirt, she could afford a room later, if she still liked the way he felt by then.

The beat slowed, and a more sensual sound came rippling from the emitters. He gently turned her around and Aspen leaned against him. Boro was shorter than she thought, and she was wearing high heels – a monstrous invention, but they gave her extra height – so she was almost at eye level with him. He was smiling softly. "You look mad beautiful tonight," he said.

A glance at his shirt – a long thing that had animated black and blue flames crawling up the length of it – and thought it was a little silly, but it made her smile, and it felt nice, not cheap or rough. His hands were warm and large against her bare back, that, and his smile were a great start as far as she was concerned. She brushed his cheek gently with the backs of her fingers before locking her hands behind his neck. "This is nice," she told him before leaning in a little.

He took his chance and kissed her, his lips parting and she followed his lead, happy that he was taking the initiative. Drew, her last on-and-off-again couldn't follow a signal if it was accompanied by flood lights and power horns. Boro was kissing her soundly and she was happy with the direction her night was taking.

The music stopped suddenly and the spinning lights became bright floods. "This is a United Core Authority raid! Stay where you are and the innocent will be released!"

They stepped away from each other and Aspen saw an emergency exit over Boro's shoulder. "There! We have to get back to the ship!" The whole dance floor rushed for it, Aspen, Boro and a few other crewmen were within three metres of the nearest exit and four UCA soldiers burst through, rifles at the ready.

With a look over her shoulder Aspen saw that Sun was right behind her. "Rush them!" she called out to the crewmembers around them. To her surprise, Boro took the lead, a pulse band over his knuckles that amplified his devastating uppercut, sending the lead UCA Officer back through the doors with a concave gold chest plate. He bullied through the space left open with two other crewmembers.

A UCA Officer tried to block Aspen, and she grabbed the seam under the front of his helmet then dragged him down, rolling back and bashing his faceplate against the dance floor. His rifle went off under her legs, a near miss that left a sear mark across the backs of her thighs. The piercing sound of his pulse weapon discharging also increased the crowd's panic, and he was pressed underfoot as Aspen flipped back up onto her feet and ran in step with Sun through the door.

"Cool Angel, this is Lieutenant Dodin, we're coming back, the station is being raided," Sun said over the communicator tattooed on her wrist.

"Genan here, what's going on?" came the response from their navigator, his head appearing in a tiny hologram above her wrist. "Wait, one sec." The face disappeared.

"Bloody moron," Sun said. "We'll be stuck in clearance for days if we don't get back to the Cool Angel."

With a touch of her finger to the communication unit imprinted on her wrist, Aspen's high heels converted to thick treaded flats that held her feet firmly, the same command altered her Lieutenant's shoes, she wobbled for a moment. "Warn me next time?" Sun said.

Flashes of light through the transparent aluminium windows drew Aspen's momentary attention, and she did her best to hold her panic down as beams flashed between several swooping United Core Authority fighters and a smooth-hulled hundred-metre-long ship. The lights started going out on the rear half of the vessel, and the ion thrusters along its side flared then flickered out. "Who are they after?" Aspen said, a substitution for asking the real question on her mind; I hope they're not after me.

They came to a crossing and took the left fork towards the nearby docking port where they'd find the Cool Angel. "Where did the rest of the crew go?" Sun asked. "They should be on their way back."

"This is the last time I wear anything without built in support," Aspen said, holding her hands over her chest. The dress made her look great, but she may as well have been running naked.

The noise from the dance club goers faded to nothing as they ran down one of the lesser concourses. Bored shopkeepers, most of them selling salvage they had dug up from a nearby world, watched the pair run past. They turned a corner down an old avenue that smelled like old Formula D Food Cubes, the kind Aspen had grown used to after a year in space, and urine. They slowed to a normal walk at the sight of a group of four soldiers. They were in the thick green armour of the UCA but didn't seem to notice that they were wearing club wear, so Sun and Aspen passed without incident.

"One more corner and we'll be on the right docking ring," Sun said. "Almost home."

Aspen got a sinking feeling, used her communication screen to look over her shoulder and saw that the four soldiers were slowly following them. "We're screwed," she said as they turned the corner. "They're here for me."

Sun looked at her quizzically. "You're an Academy girl, why would they be after you?" The hallway ahead filled with soldiers, all their rifles pointed.

"This is awkward, I never went to an Academy," Aspen said, looking for any other way out of the hall. "Especially not the UCA Academy."

"We have orders to take you into custody, Aspen Dunewell, your master is paying a lot of pips for your retrieval," the lead soldier said using a scratchy amplifier.

"You're an escaped slave?" Sun asked. "You could have warned me."

Then she spotted it, a handle that would activate an emergency lifepod. It was the only option available to her. "I really meant to tell you a better way, sorry, bye," she whispered to Sun the instant before leaping for the hatch. A bright white stun bolt missed her as she scrambled and got her hand on the old yellow handle. It creaked and turned a little, then she felt the excruciating shock of a stun bolt.

02

Aspen had numb feet, hands that felt like they were asleep, she was laying on a chilly metal table. She tried to lift her arms from where they were beside her head but found metal restraints stopped them. The rustling of a baggy one-size-fits-all suit that she'd only seen on prisoners and labour slaves chafed. She opened her eyes and took in a processing room, where stasis pods, gurneys with restraints and small cages filled the room.

"Scan complete, Commander Rahca," A fellow in a green and white uniform said as he watched a wall of readouts and icons. "Nothing in her that could poison us, blow us up, and she's in relatively good health. I deactivated her dermal computer, healed some burns from a rifle shot and took care of a small tumour on her liver. I'm a little surprised, I thought these constructs were supposed to be genetically superior."

"Not this type," a woman with white hair and far too colourful makeup in a black and green uniform said. The dashes across her chest marked her as a Commander. "Welcome back to the waking world, Aspen Number Seven, you're a rare jewel." She placed a hand on Aspen's stomach lightly. "Since the servant bots and pleasure models went crazy, we've had orders to round up any runaway dolls we can find. Raises a lot of money for the UCA, money that protects the citizens you're supposed to serve."

"I'm a real person, asshole, slavery is illegal in this system."

"You may be human," the Commander said with a crooked smile, "but you were designed, grown, then sold by a company as a product. A product that was catalogued and claimed. Have always belonged to someone, and that's who we serve. Besides, the Kensan government has fallen here, the UCA control this territory."

"They still have ships, officers, their laws matter," Aspen protested as she tried to look for an escape.

"Well, you can say whatever you like, Aspen Number Seven, it doesn't change where you're going," the Commander said, holding her hand out. A small black chit was handed to her, a dermal code reader.

Aspen tried to turn away from the Commander. "Tighten the leg restraints so I can get a direct reading."

"Sure," the short technician said, making an adjustment to a slider at the bottom of the table while leering up at her. She was forced to lay flat on the table and the Commander placed the cold, small reader on her chest. After three beeps it made a triumphant chirp, and the Commander held up the chip. A holographic image of Aspen was projected, showing her as she appeared full grown. Her height, one point five metres, her weight was fifty-six kilograms, her hair colour was branded as Delightfully Light Blonde, with the Cute n' Curvy patented facial and body appearance package. The Health and Longevity rating for her model was a four point five out of ten possible marks. She knew all this information already, but seeing herself boiled down to such bare, marketable facts was still chilling.

"We were ruled as free people in nineteen Core World systems, you can't do this. You protect at least a few of those places," Aspen protested.

"You know what I'd give for the beauty you have?" the Commander said quietly. "I know you were grown, then educated using imprinting technology we can barely touch now, but God, look at her skin, her youthfulness. They locked you at twenty-one, didn't they?"

"That doesn't mean they made me to last," Aspen said, wishing she hadn't. It was the first time she admitted to being anything but a normal human for a long time. "You know the law; you can't deliver me anywhere near Loso."

"Oh, but your owner moved to her estate in Herche, in the Kerr system, and we have to follow the law there, where dolls are perfectly legal. You'll be in an obedience anklet before the day is over. Maybe some of that reward can go towards a rollback for me, do you want to know how much you're worth?"

"Fuck you!" Aspen spat at her face, sending spittle across the Commander's eye and into her hair.

"All right," Commander Rahca said, wiping her eye and smearing her cheap orange makeup. "Activate the binders in her suit and throw her into her friend's cell."

"Wait, you took Sun?" she asked, shocked. "She didn't do anything!"

"She assaulted three of my soldiers, landed two of them in the brig using nothing but her hands and feet. A few other crewmembers joined in and tried to keep us from taking you, I don't know where they got their weapons, but they made a big mess trying to save you. They're lucky they had nothing but stunners, otherwise the charges would be much worse."

"Let them go! They were just trying to protect me, they didn't even know I was a doll!"

"It's my turn to say, 'fuck you,' you little bitch. I bet they're going to put a circlet on your little sculpted head and program all that defiance out of you." She marched from the room, leaving Aspen with the technician. A pair of guards in dark green armour entered the room a moment later.

"Okay, I have to say this, it's my job, so please don't spit on me or anything," the technician said. "Anyway, you're in a binder suit, which will allow you to move normally as long as the little computer woven into it doesn't figure you're doing something to try to escape, to hurt yourself or others. If you do try to do any of that, or to disobey any of these nice guards' orders, it'll go stiff then put you into a seated, or prone position depending on what it catches you doing. Got that? Good, now don't waste your energy fighting, just follow these guys."

"Don't hurt yourself reviewing my scans," Aspen said, looking at the life sized nude images of her on the wall.

"Nice attitude," the tech said, turning away. "Take her to Dodin's cell."

"Put them in together?" the guard on the left asked.

"Commander's orders."

Aspen slipped off the table, the cheap material was already starting to make her itch right between the shoulders. Her attempt at standing still when a soldier took her arm failed when the suit actually forced her leg forward in step with his. "Oh yeah, and you're going to notice that you have to move with us while we have you slaved to our armour," the soldier said.

"So they can put you on your knees whenever they want too," Aspen said with a smirk. She'd heard that the under suits soldiers in the UCA wore could stiffen and hold them if they tried to escape the service. "Nice navy, slave-soldier."

He grabbed her chin in his hand roughly, lowering his opaque helmet to eye level. "Dolls don't talk back. Shut up and move."

This was what it was like to be someone's property, something Aspen remembered all-too-well. A year and a half away from captivity wasn't enough to erase the memories she'd collected during her childhood and adolescent years. Her urge was to resist, but binder suits didn't exactly allow for that, so she nodded as best as she could and followed the soldiers, feeling tiny sandwiched between them. The male one, who she would call Lolly, was at least two point two metres. The female one, who she would call Pop, was two metres tall, give or take a centimetre.

The walk there was boring. Not so much as a porthole along the way, and no bored prisoners or other typical brig sights or smells were visible down the white and green hallways they walked. All Aspen could guess was that they were on a ship, judging from the faint whine she could hear from a gravitational compensator buried somewhere beneath her feet.

They opened a blank white door and shoved her inside, nearly tipping her in face-first, then the metal door slid shut behind her. "I'm sorry," she said to Sun, who was in a yellow binder suit, sitting on the bed to the left. There was another small cot to the right and a flip-down toilet.

"I can't believe you're a doll," she said. "I'm sorry, free clone? What do we call your people now?"

Aspen knew that dismissive rude mood, there was disappointment and anger beneath it, and she couldn't blame the Lieutenant she'd served faithfully for a year. "You can call me Aspen," she said, dropping onto the opposite bunk and putting her head in her hands. "I should have told you weeks ago."

"Why didn't you? Were you just waiting for me to see someone who looks exactly like you?"

"Would you tell anyone you were genetically customized as a product, grown in a facility until you were the equivalent of an eight-year-old, then sold to a Countess so she could put you in cute little dresses while you served her and her guests? Besides, Aspens were a limited run, seven of us for seventy-seven million apiece. They didn't limit our mental capacities, that was a big selling point."

"Holy shit, no wonder," Sun said. "I overheard that you were important, but one of the limited editions? I'm sorry, Aspen."

The reality of what was happening started to settle on Aspen's shoulders, all the talk of value and ownership was enough to bring all the memories back. She was starting to shake and well up, but she knew she wouldn't be able to cry, her ducts were customized so that wasn't possible. Flashes of her life before rushed back – a mixture of boredom, fear, and endless servitude. There was a little happiness, but the companion who was responsible fore those memories was gone. "I'm so sorry you got sucked into this, you should have just left me."

Sun crossed the room and knelt in front of her, laying an arm across her shoulders. "Hey, I know you wouldn't have left me. You've been my second for almost a year, and I've never felt like anyone had my back more than you."

"You're going to prison, or to a work camp, maybe even hers, since the UCA can't afford to keep more than one prison open. They'll probably sell you to the Countess."

"Why are you so afraid of her?"

"There are only three things you have to know about the Countess," Aspen said, raising her face from its nest in her hands and looking into Sun's green eyes. "First, she's crazy. You don't know what she'll be in the mood for from one moment to the next. Second, she does not understand sympathy or mercy. The pain she causes other people isn't real to her. Third, and this is why she can boss the UCA around, she's so wealthy that she can afford to lose three of her moons, move house across the sector, and buy governments without losing a minute's sleep. I've seen one of her vaults, and there was so much molecularly stamped platinum in there that the thing was cracking the granite base it was on."

"How?"

"Her family, her slave network and who knows how many heavy metal extraction outposts. She even has manual labour farms where they grow coffee, vanilla, cinnamon, all those extra-expensive food things that boutiques sell as the genuine article."

"What, does she own Omni Natural Foods or something?" Sun asked.

"That's one of the big ones," Aspen said. "I escaped when the household droids turned on us. My companion was killed, I thought she was dead too, so I took the opportunity and just ran. If she's alive, and I get within her walls, I'll never be free again, so forget me. Forget me forever and try to escape. I only have two years left anyway, but you made one of 'em better than I could have imagined. I liked serving under you, even though our Captain was a pain in the ass."

"Yeah, I'm pretty sure he sold you out," Sun said, sitting on the floor at Aspen's feet. "It's the only thing that makes sense. Something he'd do for a quick payday too."

"I'm going to slit his throat when I get free," Aspen said, certain that it could never happen. No one ever escaped from the Countess twice.

"Only if I don't shove him out an airlock first. Wait, back up, what do you mean, 'you only have two years left?'"

"Yeah, that's the problem with my model. We only last so long before we get really sick all of a sudden and die. I've kept my eyes open for a gene therapy, done research, but we haven't run into anything that looks like a solution, it's pretty tamper-proof. They let us be as smart and as healthy as any human, but for a limited time only."

"There has to be someone, or some lab somewhere that could do something?" Sun asked.

Aspen caressed her friend's face, cupping a cheek in her hand. "Thank you so much for being good to me for a year, you know how much that means now, right? When you don't have much time, what you do counts. We might have been thieving and smuggling, but I had so much fun doing it beside you. I've got about two years left, and the only place that might have a solution is the place where I was made. Problem is, New Skin's facility is deep in crazy robot territory, I'll be surprised if there's a human alive in the Geist system."

"Geist? It had to be Geist?" Sun said, staring up at her for a long moment. "No, there's a solution, something.

We get out of this, we meet where we found all those old ships and then we fix you, okay? That's what's going to happen."

Aspen knew what she was talking about. When they were robbing a station that turned into a death trap after the artificial intelligence turned on the occupants they found a whole room filled with ancient ships in bottles. Sun delivered the best one to Captain White, and the last time Aspen saw it, it was under the small table in the Captain's quarters collecting dust. "With all the old ships, yeah, I'll meet you there."

The door shifted to the side suddenly and Aspen was dragged out then shoved down the hall to the next door. Commander Rocha stepped into the doorway after she was dumped into an even smaller room. "The place with all the ships? What are you talking about? Where are you planning to meet?"

"Olega, the Starfire Shipyards have a museum there," Aspen said. "Guess that plan's done for." It was two sectors in the opposite direction from Kwalli Station.

"Neither of you are getting away, this is the UCA, you stupid little thing," the Commander said, shaking her head. "Idiot. Keep her here until we arrive. Put her out, no need for her to be conscious."

"Good God, I need to murder you," Aspen said, meaning every syllable.

Commander Rehea paused a moment, staring at her prisoner in shock. "I don't think God hears dolls, now do they?" the door closed as soon as she finished her taunt.

Aspen tried to lunge forward but the suit stopped her. She felt a sharp pinch on her arm then the room began to fade. With a crooked grin, Aspen turned herself so her head was perfectly in line with the edge of the flip down toilet, which was stuck in the open position. "Wonder if the suit can stop this?" she asked before losing consciousness, leaning forward.

03

The powerful aroma of lilacs struck Aspen's senses as she woke. It was the last thing she wanted to smell, it meant that the Countess was near. Opening her eyes and sitting up, she realized that she was aboard a simple small transport with three rows of plush, reclining seats. It was the Fleet Feather, a ship that was gilded on the inside and outside, with a pattern of fine interlocking branches drawn across the interior in platinum leaf. Wood trimming was everywhere, and the intelligent seating was upholstered with organically produced cloth. The outside of the ship always reminded Aspen of a broad-breasted bird that was about to take flight, if a bird could be red and purple. As one of the former keepers of the Countess' accounts, she knew the vessel was worth more than most luxury estates, and the upkeep was even more expensive.

This was the main transport vehicle for the Countess' least important guests. It doubled as an escort craft, with a few extra guns, and she'd seen most of the inside, but always travelled with the Countess herself on her craft. The cockpit was a mystery. She knew it was up the stairs in the main forward hallway, after the crew quarters and the small galley, but the hatch was always locked up there.

That damned binding suit was holding her in place, so she was sitting perfectly upright in the middle of the seating area. There was no sign of her crewmates, only two guards who wore the gilded armour that marked them as servants of the Countess's house. The white plate would be more intimidating if it wasn't adorned with gold and bronze filigree, making them look dainty.

The ship touched down with a brief chorus of creaks and the cockpit door opened. "Right, ramp's down, unload quick now," bellowed the pilot from above before he slammed the hatch again.

The guards approached and Aspen's suit relaxed its hold on her. The search for any opportunity to escape began then. "On your feet, if you please. We do not want to clean up another mess, so don't injure yourself again."

"Oh, the suit didn't stop me from falling?" Aspen asked, a little amused. "Cracked my head open?"

"The UCA treated you, but we had to clean the blood off your suit. There was a lot. Please move carefully."

Aspen knew that the guards were usually nice to her as long as she didn't break the rules. Sometimes they'd even let her bend them as a child, though she was sure she'd have to re-earn their trust after being away for over a year. She followed them out of the secondary hold and let them guide her down the narrow corridor, watching for unlocked hatches, open crawlspaces or a control panel that she could quickly mess with to shake them, but didn't find anything on her way to the ramp leading off the ship. The smell of fresh lilacs blasted her in the face as she set foot on a cobblestone courtyard. Its paths were lined with the purple flowering trees.

The Countess's new palace was even more grand than the last one. Marble and ancient brick walkways arched from the ground paths leading through a massive garden to a broad elevated marble platform. Spraying fountains with cherubs and stone beasts chasing barely dressed maidens adorned the massive central platform along with benches, several tables and bars attended by beautiful servants. A long polished stone concourse led from there to the main building, a tall structure with pillars across the front. Black vines climbed the façade behind them and the main doors were adorned with white and yellow gold. There was nothing subtle about her old master.

"Aspen?" asked a familiar voice. Aspen's mood brightened as Larken ran from the grass to her left and embraced her. His long blonde hair was soft and silky, he reeked of lilacs. The oil that had been brushed into his hair was worse than the trees. He gave her a kiss on the cheek and held her at arm's length. "You look good," he said, surprised. "The Countess said you joined a band of pirates, that you were no better than a street rat. I was worried."

"I was free, Larken," she said. "I would have taken you with me, I thought you were dead."

"I was protecting the Countess, who is fine now, by the way. She had to spend a week visiting the flesh crafters, then there was recovery, but she's brave, and pulled through."

"I don't care about her, I'm just glad to see you. I ran because I thought you were dead. When I didn't get caught using my real name, I was sure the Countess was dead too. I don't think there was a day when I didn't wish you were free with me," Aspen said. The last part was true until only a few months before. She couldn't remember when exactly she started thinking about her future without him, but she did, and life started to get better. Seeing him alive brought a rush of love, regret, and relief. She almost didn't notice that he nearly flinched every time she mentioned freedom, or running away. He was her favourite person, they were made together, to be a genetic match as a couple for their entire short lives. Why she loved him didn't matter, whether it started when they were created in a lab or was brought on by a mystical force, the feeling that she had to be with him was stronger than any sensation she'd ever felt. If she didn't think he was dead, she would have never left.

Aspen tried to embrace him but she was stopped short by the suit. He wrapped his arms around her and she squeezed him as much as she was allowed to once they were cheek to cheek. "I was torn apart," she whispered against his ear. He shushed her and said; "it's all right, you're where you belong now."

Aspen was chilled by the thought of what may come, and inwardly cursed herself for not realizing that the thought that she didn't want to be brought back hadn't even occurred to Larken. She stepped back, steeling herself.

Larken regarded her wordlessly for a moment then as his expression betrayed his disappointment. "You've changed so much," he said quietly. "The Countess won't be happy, but I'm glad you're back. I missed you so much, Aspen. I'm sure she did too, you'll just have to earn her trust, it's going to take some time, but we owe her that much, right?"

It made Aspen furious to see Larken so obedient, he was much worse than before, but she hid it, and nodded her response.

He took her hand, the long sleeve of his loose silk robe complicating the gesture for a moment, and smiled at her. "Good, let's see if she's ready for you to attend to her. She's so anxious to see you again that she told me to wait for you and present you just as you are, so you'll have to bathe and change after."

"Here we go," she said, eying the perimeter of the massive garden as he whirled towards the platform ahead. His black, gold and white decorated robe billowed in the breeze, and he took a moment to adjust it a little. The thing was open down the middle of his chest, coming to a close at his waist. Tight black leggings and sandals completed his simple outfit, exactly the kind of thing a doll would wear.

A glow in the distance to her left and right indicated that there was some kind of energy shield surrounding the garden. There were also no designated spaces for sliders or any other ground vehicles, meaning that they were probably blocked or far from any civilized outpost. If the only way in was by ship, she would have to find out where the new hangar was and steal one. If the shield surrounded the entire complex, she'd have even more work to do.

"Do you know where my friends were taken?" she asked as she walked hand-in-hand with Larken.

"Those people?" he asked. "The vineyard always needs people, so probably there. Why? Do you think any of them would be suitable to serve at court?"

"One, she's dark haired, named Sun," Aspen replied. She hadn't even thought of suggesting that someone who was captured with her could be transferred to the slave pool for court. It was a long shot at best, and presenting the idea would have to happen at the right time. "Let's wait to mention it though, I'd rather have all the attention on me while we're celebrating my return."

"So you missed court? You missed the Countess?" Larken asked, brightening.

"I missed you," she said. "Maybe some of the clothes, my bed, but I missed you constantly." His mood was descending as she spoke so she added; "Of course I missed the Countess, she's like a mother to me, only better."

"Good, I'll tell her, make sure she knows you agree that leaving was a mistake."

Anger boiled deep within her, the servants they passed averted their gazes as she walked by. They moved across the platform between the garish fountains and tables filled with ultra-rich guests who wore the most outrageous outfits. Aspen didn't see any of the servants or slaves she knew, and wondered if they survived the chaos as the machines turned on them, or if they managed to use the opportunity to escape like she did. Those were mysteries she could solve later.

The main foyer of the palace was four stories tall with a polished black floor that was polished to a reflective gloss. The alcoves along the walls featured many of the fashion triumphs enjoyed by the Countess. Once upon a time, when Aspen was still a child, she would look at those in wonder, marvelling at the creativity and beauty. They looked silly, and overly decadent to her now. Some of the dresses were so complex that the Countess had to be carried from place to place, others had multiple trains that drifted off the ground thanks to some kind of device hidden in the folds of the cloth, and the most embarrassing one – Aspen's favourite for that very reason – reached up for several metres in fluted lengths of white fabric that came back down again, drooping like a willow tree around the Countess, who always had difficulty maintaining her balance in the outfit.

Four guards in gilded armour regarded Larken and her as they approached the tallest set of double doors Aspen had ever seen. They were decorated with real gold and platinum filigree that joined in the centre to form the Countess's house crest – a vine with grapes, a new born and a shield hanging from it. The only symbol that seemed to suit the countess was the grapes, as far as Aspen was concerned.

This was the main audience chamber, she knew it, and Aspen took one last look around for any means of escape. At a quick count there were two guards standing behind each pillar along the foyer, making for at least fourteen in the room, and they had all the doors covered. There was no way out, she'd have to put up with the horrible creature again.

"This is our Aspen, returned to us after a long absence," Larken said. "The Countess wanted to see her right away."

"That's not Aspen, you're joking. Her hair's not the right colour, and Aspen would never be so filthy," one guard said, looking her up and down.

"Tell her we have arrived," Larken insisted.

One of the guards turned his head, the underside of his jaw moving, he was talking into his helmet communicator. They moved aside, the guard who assessed Aspen guiding her and Larken to the side. "Behind the screen, please," she said, directing them to a screen in an alcove beside the door that perfectly blended in with the finish on the walls. The pair waited there, listening to the sound of the grand doors sliding open with a rumble, then dozens of footsteps walking past.

Larken never let go of her hand, and he tugged it to get her attention. "I don't know if I will have a chance to say this any time soon, but I didn't realize how much I loved you until you were gone. I'm so sorry I didn't act on it sooner, but they always had people watching us as we were about to come of age."

Aspen was about to placate him, but his lips were planted on hers before she had a chance. They were raised together like a pair of swans destined to be paired for life, and he was her best friend growing up. She always thought he was comely before, even used to watch him when she thought he wasn't looking but after he died – or rather, after she thought he died – she mourned, and eventually allowed herself to start noticing other men. Before long, she realized her tastes leaned towards more masculine fellows, a scar was a story to her, callouses were a sign of a hard worker, and imperfections made some people seem more interesting. She still thought Larken was appealing, but in a way that was perhaps pretty, not handsome. He was emasculated by the cut of his robe, his perfect long hair, and the makeup that blushed his cheeks and accentuated his blue eyes. She'd long since abandoned the quest for cosmetic perfection. Her daily regimen included bathing, and a little colour or gloss on her lips when it wore off.

His advance wasn't entirely unwelcome, however, and she let him kiss her, his lips softening against hers as he realized he wasn't about to be pushed away. He tasted of peaches, and moved his lips slowly, prying, lightly pinching hers. It was much more like the time Sun and her kissed on a lark to tease a few of their crewmembers at a party than anything else. He kissed as sweetly as Sun did, but less firmly. Aspen liked it, she loved Larken even though he still seemed to love the Countess, so she returned the kiss, adding vigour to it, and she licked his tongue forward to play for a moment before gently closing her lips and withdrawing with a smile. "I love you too, Larken," she whispered, feeling a sharp pang of guilt. "I don't think the Countess would be okay with this though."

"I don't know. A lot has changed. Things have been strange since we received news that you were recovered, she has been very particular about how I look. There's some kind of consultant named Panna at court, she scans me often and reports to the Countess in private. Neither of them seem happy about whatever they're talking about."

"I might know what it's about, but it'll have to wait," Aspen said. "Help me get back into the Countess's good graces. I can't bear how angry she's going to be when she sees me," she said, applying years of stage craft thanks to endless drama lessons.

"Oh, no," Larken said, full of concern. "She adores you, this is a cause for great celebration."

"The Countess will see you now, come this way," a tall shapeshifter said. His upper body was a long taper with vertical eyes that protruded slightly, dragging brown-yellow skin with them when they peered here and there.

"Thank you, Seneschal," Larken said.

Aspen didn't have much time to adjust to the fact that their old Seneschal had been replaced, he'd been a kind man who doted on her while she was at court. "What happened to Arsenault?"

"He was killed by the artificial intelligence controlling the kitchen," Larken said.

"Oh my God," Aspen said. "I hope it was quick."

"It was not. I had to help clean, I don't want to talk about it," Larken said.

They entered the great hall, where the Countess held audience, and the theme of stone pillars in front of walls with deep alcoves was repeated, only the stone was crimson, brown and grey. At the end was a single tall throne that wove those colours together using vines riddled with gemstones. A seven step dais held it above everyone in the grand chamber, where holograms of the Countess' ancestors haunted the alcoves. Above those alcoves were tall windows, blue skies and a few spiral stone spires were visible but nothing else. Upon the throne sat Countess Valona Tineau Danti. Her garb was surprisingly simple – a long blue gown with a black under layer that showed through down the centre. Fine platinum chains hung down the backs of her long sleeves, sliding against the throne as she stood.

Flesh crafting had made the woman unnaturally thin and tall. Her face was always narrow and long, but it seemed even more so with a neck extended at least twice that of a normal humans, lengthened arms, legs, narrow hips and a waist that looked like stretched toffee. Special muscle groups, an extended spine and outer support that were added by the flesh crafters while they were making alterations kept it all together. A shock of white hair made her head look even taller, a lattice work jutting up from the shoulders of her dress held the locks aloft for her.

The Countess was hundreds of years old, the flesh crafting had been taking place well before Aspen or anyone she knew were born. Her family were far, far away, Aspen had never knowingly met any of them, but she knew that the Countess sat far above them in the hierarchy. Outside of her palaces, the woman was universally despised, but she could utterly destroy anyone in her considerable sphere of influence, and Aspen saw it happen more than once while she stood beside that throne. The Countess used the law, blackmail, her own corporate empires, even her own private military to destroy her enemies. She did so often, and with pleasure.

"The little Autumn returns," the Countess purred, her tailored voice high pitched but soft. A woman in a simpler, long crimson dress holding a slim, high powered hand scanner walked alongside the Countess. The device cost as much as some small freighters, and it was pointed at Aspen. "What have you done to yourself, girl?" she looked to the guards. "Get that off of her immediately."

A button on the back of her collar was pressed and the suit reverted to its inert sheet state, falling off. Aspen caught it just in time, holding it to her bosom but the Countess yanked it off of her and flung it across the room with her inhumanly long fingers. Larken started taking his robe off only to be pushed to the side. "Keep your clothes on, stupid boy," the Countess said. "I don't need you for comparison, I can see she's ruined you as a matched pair, she may as well be some freakish alien. I'll still inspect her personally, the damage must be assessed."

"Yes, Countess," Larken said, bowing deeply and straightening his clothes.

This was the essence of what Aspen hated about her life under the Countess. Nothing was hers, even her body was property. The Countess flicked a lock of hair. "Such a common brown colour," her hand ran down her back.

"Pasty pale, and so fat. It is as though you have been hiding under a stone from the sun, getting fat on grubs and worms. Where have you been, child?"

Aspen waited for the inspection to continue, not expecting that she was being called on to answer a question so soon after entering her presence.

"Answer me, girl!" the Countess shrieked, her voice not so smooth or pretty.

"They kept me on a ship, where I had to carry cargo," Aspen said, the answer was ready at hand thanks to many terrible daydreams where she imagined she was recaptured. "It was very hard."

"I don't believe you," the Countess said, leaning forward so she could try and look Aspen in the eyes. "They found you at a dance club, you were dressed like a commoner who was looking to breed with some thuggish thing, the way you were writhing against him. I have the footage, but I could barely stand watching it, my stomach is still unsettled. What do you have to say for yourself?"

"I'm sorry, I won't leave you again," Aspen said as pleadingly as she could.

The woman in the crimson dress tsked and shook her head at the Countess.

"Lying little bitch," the Countess hissed. "You've gone pale, and chubby," she said, cruelly pinching skin and a little flesh from Aspen's belly and twisting, pulling. "You should be bronze, just like Larken and beautifully blonde, innocent creatures of nature. It's what I paid for!"

Aspen suppressed the urge to slap the Countess's hand away, her face turned red by the time she was released.

"Hair grown too long, and missing entirely in other places, it's as if you don't realize how much work it was to have you made. You're too stupid to realize how perfect you were! Where there was texture and perfect shape, you've bulged and made yourself plain. You 're not meant to change at a whim like some…" she struggled to find the word.

Nothing had ever made her angrier than what was going on right at that instant, and even worse, Larken was cowering several metres away, not enraged but terrified. "Like a doll?" Aspen finished for the Countess.

"No," the Countess said, whirling at her, pointing a long, thin finger. "You are common, but we will restore you. Consider yourself fortunate that I am willing to overlook your defiance, and that I don't have to call my flesh crafters to fix what you have done. By this evening you will be standing in your place beside my right coffer. Poor Larken has not been able to take his place at my left hand because it would have set the whole dais off balance, and we even tried to match him with another Aspen, number three. It was a disaster! They had no chemistry, even after months. I tried everything, but it was all fumbling and polite misunderstandings and failed attempts at romance. I even tried to make the match work by killing that Aspen's mate, but the girl wouldn't stop moping. A few weeks later she managed to get her hands on a grenade, put it in her mouth and set it off in the garden. We were having an outdoor luncheon! The Duchess of Mir lost an arm, and she still won't stop talking about it. It was such an expensive waste, but why should I even bring that up to you two, you barely know what money is!"

Aware that the hand scanner was pointed at her and that her lies would be detected, Aspen gathered all the emotion she could. "I'm so sorry, Countess," she said and she was sorry, but only that she was recaptured. The weight of the situation couldn't be more clear to her, and she couldn't feel more forlorn or afraid.

The Countess glanced at the woman in the crimson dress, who shrugged, then regarded Aspen. "You are telling the truth, Aspen," she said, slightly awed. "Was it so terrible being away from court?"

"Yes," Aspen said, focusing on how awful it was to be back.

"Then your repentance may be short, especially if you are obedient in the coming weeks. Larken, give her your tunic and bring her to my own cosmetic aides, they'll set her right again. Oh, and signal the kitchen. She's on a strict diet starting immediately, it must be horrible having so much extra weight to drag around. I understand this, perhaps," the Countess said, waving in the general direction of Aspen's chest. Then she pinched her hip and her belly, less cruelly but still sharply. "But this extra matter, and those thick thighs. It's like looking at some fat, plucked flightless bird."

Aspen poured extra effort into smiling at Larken as he wrapped his robe around her. "But look," the Countess said, smiling for the first time since their reunion began. "My summer pair are back together again. You still match, despite Aspen's unfortunate self mutilation."

04

Bright, penetrating lights were everywhere in the palace beauty parlour. Aspen had blissfully forgotten the ridiculous regimen that she and Larken had to follow to look the way their creators – those capitalist genetic designers – had advertised. She felt as though she had never left once the stylists and specialists descended on her, dressed in white and blue smocks.

Eyebrows and hair were follicle adjusted so they grew at the right matching pace and colour, then everything was colour shifted to match the lively highlighted blonde colour she was supposed to have. The follicles Aspen had adjusted to her liking everywhere else were reactivated so she would have more, and then they were stimulated so, after a few minutes of furious itching, she was 'reforested' as one of the smiling technicians said. Aspen was not amused. "What about my legs? Natural women have hairy legs," she said, thrusting a calf up from her seat.

The technician looked at the bare limb, then to the the beauticians to either side, and in half a panic she asked; "Is that in the design?" Another beautician brought up a hologram of Aspen's legs and shook his head. "Then it doesn't go on you, dear. We must stick to the blueprint."

"You realize I'm going to be dead in two years anyway, right? Like a switch going off, I'll get painfully sick, my organs will take about a week to fail, and then I'll be another corpse buried in the back garden, rotting under the lilac trees," Aspen said, creating the deepest uncomfortable silence she'd ever seen, it was fantastic. "I've got an expiry date so all this is really pretty pointless."

"Let's try to keep our composure, luv," the eldest of the technicians said, plucking an errant hair from her neck. "This will take much longer if you bring dark clouds into the room."

There was no escape, not for the moment, Aspen reminded herself silently. Sometimes the only way out was through, not around, not up or over, so she went against every instinct she had for the rest of the day. "I'm sorry, you all work very hard, thank you."

"Well, thank you," the only male one said, he was one of the so-called technicians, which meant he handled the more invasive devices. "We honestly don't hear that enough."

The next hour was one Aspen wished she could forget. Even when they were finished and rubbing a special blend of lotions into her skin – the reward for all the rest – she knew it wasn't really at an end. The assembly line went on, the makeup artists got to work on her next. To Aspen's chagrin, the Countess had something special planned that night, and she was to be made up in brown and green dye.

"You mean body paint?" she asked when one of the artists informed her.

"No, my girl, take that robe off. We are to paint you like a wood nymph from ancient lore from head to toe. The presentation for your second debut will be a work of art. Nothing can run, nothing can drip, so it's brushes and dyes for you. Hold still please." Those were the last words spoken for a long time as the lead makeup artist and five of his assistants painted her until she looked like some child of the woods. It took two hours for them to do what a bot would have done in fifteen minutes if it were the old days.

They kept her robe as she was sent on to the next stage, where she hoped they'd dress her, since all she was wearing was green, brown and black dyes. They covered her from head to toe so she looked like she was made from grass and trees but still very feminine – enough so she wished there was a bush she could hide in – so she hoped it was just undercoating.

"Well, they certainly did their best," a tall woman covered in fine silver fur sighed. She was of a race Aspen had never seen before, but she liked the big eyes and long, pink nose tipped snout. "I'm sorry dear, your frock is to be very simple tonight, the Countess wants to show you off. Court has been boring this season."

A soft brown and green cloak was wrapped around her shoulders, cloth twigs and leaves were sewn into the garment. The tall furry woman regarded her for a moment, tilting her head and looking at the robe. "It fits, and it hides all but your neck and face, exactly as the Countess ordered."

"Then why did I just get painted?"

"That is an excellent question that I can't answer, my dear. I'm Tonic."

"It's good to meet you," Aspen replied.

"I'll be dressing you until you eventually escape," she replied in a whisper. "Don't say anything, I just know that's how your time here will end. There is something about you that tells me that this won't last long."

Aspen raised the sides of her cloak high enough to surround her face so only Tinick could see her and mouthed; "Can you help me?"

Tinick laughed cheerily and shook her head. "I'm from the theatre, a place where we understand the importance of timing, you understand. If someone comes in too early, they embarrass themselves, too late and they show a kind of unprofessionalism that leads to even deeper humiliation. When treading the boards of a great house, either one is akin to death. If there's any help I can offer, it's only a lesson in timing."

The message was fairly clear to Aspen, she had to time whatever she did just right, wait for the right opportunity and make sure she didn't miss it. She decided that she could help hide the tip by asking a clever question. "Am I part of any performances tonight? Is there anything I shouldn't miss? I'd hate to make things worse by disappointing the Countess even more."

"You are an ornament this evening, the Countess is only interested in showing the court that you have returned, but she doesn't want anyone to see that you've changed. You know, I think you look healthier than the one who was dieted and primped to specification, but what do I know? I've only been designing and costuming for thirty years. I would say stand still, pay attention, and try not to fall asleep on your feet."

"So, all I'm getting is this robe, and I'll be standing there all night," Aspen said. "Dais deco mode."

"As far as I know," Tinick said, tugging the hood up and fixing it into place. "Our time is finished for today, I'll see you tomorrow morning. I'm supposed to make you look unrealistically skinny using nothing but my wits and clothing, so that's something you can look forward to." The silver furred creature rolled her eyes and shook her head.

Aspen left the room, looking forward to seeing the new designer again, but not looking forward to whatever measures it might take to create the illusion that she hadn't gained weight since she escaped. It irked her that she would be forced to lose centimetres, she felt healthy, and no one ever complained about her appearance when she was free.

The ball was already under way, and palace guards met Aspen as soon as she emerged from the wardrobe room with her cloak closed all the way down. There was nothing but dye underneath, and Aspen wasn't interested in putting a show on before she had to. Her stomach grumbled. There had been plenty to drink, some of it thick and sweet, not much of it identified, but it seemed that within minutes of her mouth leaving a straw, hunger began creeping back.

Following the guards to the side entrance of the ball room, she asked them; "neither of you would have anything to eat on you, would you? I'll flash a little leg for half a meal bar, c'mon."

The guard on the left chuckled, the other shook his head.

"I'll open right up for a hot Power Pocket," she added, opening the top of her robe a few centimetres.

The one who shook his head slipped her a meal bar and said; "No flashing required. You didn't get that from me, right?"

"You are my saviour, and its bad luck to rat on someone who saves your butt," Aspen said as she hid it in the neck of her robe and took a big bite. They were in the narrow side entrance to the ball room, waiting for a red light to go on above their heads. "You get double points for chocolate, oh my God, thank you." She said through a full mouth.

"Hurry up and scarf that down," the other guard said, chuckling.

The bar was gone too soon, but she was happy to have had solid food without getting caught. "Thanks again, um, which one are you?"

"No names," he replied. "That way I won't get fired or killed over a meal bar."

"Good point."

The light above her head turned red and the doors opened silently, cool mist rolling in front of it. The lights in the ball room were dimmed, and Aspen could see the stars through the tall windows at the other end of the hall.

There was a clear lane between hundreds of gathered guests leading to the middle of the massive vaulted room. Dead leaves lined the aisles with faint green light between. Aspen saw that Larken was already approaching from the other side of the hall, horns protruding from his head, brown dye and paints applied so he looked like he belonged in some ancient woodland. He was more muscular than she remembered, and Aspen hoped that the costumer was right, that there was nothing special planned for her that night.

When they met in the middle, Larken gently took her in his arms. "A little kiss," he said before planting his lips on hers for a lingering moment, then he walked her to the foot of the Countess's throne. "I present your Aspen, once lost in the wild, now found and returned," he said to her.

Aspen followed his lead as he bowed deeply. All Aspen could see were the Countess's green-shod feet, she was bowing so low, and for a long moment she remained frozen in place.

"Welcome home," was all the Countess had to say to set the courtiers off in a torrent of polite clapping. The sound made her cringe, but Aspen made sure she was smiling brightly when the Countess' long fingers touched her forehead, then directed her and Larken to take their places to her right and left.

Given a moment of quiet, even from the right side of the dais, Aspen's thoughts returned to the crewmembers who were delivered to the Countess because they tried to help her. She couldn't help but wonder where her friends were, what they were doing, and how she'd get them out of the mess she'd gotten them into.

The membership of the Countess' court was a mixture of the military, government, and social elite. It had been too long, and the mad machines had killed too many of the old wealthy courtiers, or at least that's the assumption Aspen made. She didn't recognize any of the faces out of the two hundred or more people in the massive space. In the dim light, she only saw clothes stuffed with unfamiliar humans. United Core Authority uniforms socialized with revealing dresses and tight summer suits, while less fashionable suits and dresses adorned with government seals mixed between awkwardly. These were the people who had to work harder to find their way to the social elite, the ones that were elected, or planted, or controlled and generally disrespected by everyone else. She'd seen it before. Few government officials had the respect of the ultra-wealthy or the highest ranks in the military. Either group could have someone in government replaced, but it wasn't so easy to supplant the wealthy or the military.

The faces were different, but the dynamic was the same, leading Aspen to wonder if she would find a friendly maverick amongst them. There was always at least one person who thought differently, respected life more than the rest, and would bend the rules for the sake of doing something different. They were often easy to spot either because they were more flamboyant or deeply, obviously bored. She had to find them fast, earn their trust or at least intrigue them enough to get their help. Her friends were waiting, and she didn't want to put up with the Countess' lifestyle for a minute longer than she had to.

The revelation that Larken was alive made everything complicated. If it weren't for him she would take the first chance she had to slip away and get the information she needed from the computer. At the next opportunity, she'd steal a ship and do whatever she could to get her friends, but Larken was still deluded to think that he was living a good life with the Countess, that she saw him as something other than property.

Every time she looked into his eyes she wanted to kiss him, and she wanted to slap him. He seemed dazed to her, like she just needed the right words or the right image to wake him from his daydream and then they could leave together. There were layers of security, faithful courtiers that could get in their way, but if her taste of freedom taught her anything, it was that luck favoured decisive people who took the initiative. She'd find her way out, she'd find the right time, and Aspen hoped she could convince Larken to go with her when it came.

Her thoughts were interrupted as one of the courtiers, an older woman started crossing the empty space between the dais and her. She was in a simpler dress that celebrated new blooms with bits of fabric hanging off like leaves and flower petals all the way down. It was equipped with a hood that the woman kept half up and toyed with. "Are you in there, Aspen?" she asked, smiling.

Aspen recognized her voice right away. "Instructor Emani? You look very healthy tonight," she said, priding herself on replacing the word 'young' with 'healthy' the instant before she said it. Her old instructor in most things from politics, to finances, to life skills looked twenty years younger than she did when Aspen was eight.

"It's a long story, but I was caught in the attack that nearly killed the Countess and they decided to give me more years while I was in recovery. It's good to see you healthy and whole, Aspen."

"I used-" Aspen corrected herself before going on. "I was forced to use so much of what you taught me while I was away. I don't think I would have survived if I didn't spend years learning from you."

"Flatterer," she said. "I should have you speak to the new ones I'm teaching. They're more fitful than you were at that age. Do you think you may need some brushing up? We could do both at the same time."

"That sounds good, I would serve much better if I could catch up on what's been happening while I've been gone. I'm sure a lot has changed," Aspen said. There was no sign that her instructor was hinting at anything more than she was saying, though she watched her every move just in case the older woman had some tip for her.

"It's set then, tomorrow afternoon unless something comes up for you," Instructor Emani said. "Good to see you again," she said before drifting back towards the crowd.

Broad trays piled high with tasty morsels were brought in from the left and right entrances. They moved past the dais, to the Countess first, then to Larken and Aspen. She was just looking forward to taking a cream filled strawberry when the Countess looked to the servers. "She doesn't need anything tonight."

Aspen remained in her place stoically as she watched the server with the first fruit tray regard her with sympathy before moving on to the rest of the room. She flashed him a brief smile, knowing that his lot was much worse than hers. The slave quarters were a place of harsh discipline and hard work.

Watching the crowd of guests socialize, dance but most of all eat and drink started to get on Aspens' nerves before long. The first thing she complained about when she won her freedom was the immediate reduction in the quality of the food, that was, until she ran out. She faced real starvation and dehydration a few times in the early days, but once she joined the crew of the Cool Angel her food and water worries came to an end. There was a lot to complain about there, but she never found herself without some kind of food within reach. Compared to most crewmembers, she ate very little, so much so her Lieutenant, Sun often encouraged her to eat more.

"I think I'll retire for the evening," the Countess said. She had spoken to only five courtiers, and didn't mingle at all, something that surprised Aspen. When she was in service before, her throne was constantly surrounded, the chattering used to remind her of a hen house from the organic ranch. A look at the new courtiers suggested that they may be afraid of the Countess, or perhaps shied by her appearance.

Even her consort, Kort, was absent. Aspen silently hoped he was killed when the machines turned. She also hoped that she wouldn't be pressed into socializing on the Countess' behalf. As Larken and her approached adulthood they were pressed into service as negotiators and general socializers in her court. Most of the people she met were vain, proud and in search of praise or some other prize. Some would proposition her tirelessly, something Larken had to put up with only a little less. A few became friends, and she found none in the crowd that night.

"You may both retire," the Countess said as she carefully stood and exited using a special door hidden behind her throne. Her dress was surprisingly unremarkable, white with blue highlights that flowed down the extensive length.

The courtiers didn't seem to pay much attention to the Countess's departure. Larken was at her side, taking her hand the moment the door sealed behind the Countess. He led her from the hall into a servant's corridor. "Where are we going?" Aspen asked.

"I'm taking you to my rooms, I can't wait to spend time away with you, and to get this dye off," he said as he rushed through the narrower corridors with their scuffed walls and floors. Servants dressed in loose white tunics and gold leggings let them pass as they held trays piled with drinks.

Aspen couldn't help but snatch two high, frosty, fruity glasses. The slave, a girl just old enough to serve, smiled at her, amused by the theft. Larken stopped and looked back at Aspen when her hand slipped from his and she gave him one of the stolen drinks.

"We don't have much time," Larken whispered in a tone that was much more serious than any he'd used that day.

She kept up, carrying the drinks as carefully as she could as they cut through one of the kitchens, where she was tempted to put them down and trade up for anything being prepared there. Stealing from the kitchen would be harder than a drink tray, however, the slaves there took more pride in their work than the servers, and they had paid chefs as keepers who might notice.

A few turns through the halls later, and they reached the main rooms, where silent attendants stood at the ready to serve any of the residents in that wing. All one had to do was use the intercom inside a room and one of the platinum and gold clad attendants would assist you with whatever you liked. The rewards for the post were generous, but Aspen heard stories about what some of them had to deliver, take away or do inside the rooms to assist some of

50

the more eccentric and demanding guests. She would rather de-grease an entire space station's gear works than take the job of a household attendant.

Larkin's room was lavish, and surprisingly adult. Any artefacts of his childhood were absent, including the plushie horse he used to sleep with as a child, or any evidence of fandom. There were no images on the wall, just their favourite colours – crimson and royal blue – on the walls, decorating the bed, and in the trimming. The main room had a lavish bed, an adjacent closet larger than most small shuttle craft, and a bathroom that was larger than any crew quarters she'd ever seen.

He took the drinks from her politely, put them down on an end table, then pulled her into his arms. "Trust me," he whispered against her lips before kissing her and slowly pulling her robe down.

Aspen found him irresistible, especially since there seemed to be much more firmness in his kiss. She didn't just relent, she joined him vigorously, letting her robe drop and pulling at the ties holding his up.

With a sudden jerk that made her yip and giggle, he picked her up and carried her into the large shower with him. Warm water sprayed from all angles and a vibration system forced it to gently scrub their skin. He held her close after putting her down, and kissed her briefly before smiling at her. It was a real, open smile, the kind only she could get out of him. "We can talk here, the listening devices can't pick anything up with the vibrating micro-beads running in the shower. The Countess told me you were killed when the AI's turned on us. She even showed me video and had a funeral. I found out you were alive three months ago, when Master Kort let it slip that he was hunting you. It was so hard to hide how angry I was, but I had to keep the Countess' trust," he said in a rush. He caressed her back and shoulders as he did so, and she watched him speak. The deluded version of Larken, who worshipped the Countess was completely gone. "When she told me you were alive yesterday, that the UCA found you, I finally revealed that I had known for months. I've never seen her so surprised in my life, but she trusts me even more now that she's seen that I didn't try to escape and find you myself. What was it like out there? Master Kort tells everyone that it's a lawless, no-man's land. He says raiders attack all the time, and the UCA is losing everywhere."

"It's dangerous," Aspen said. "But as soon as I met people who needed me, I started making friends, making money. Do you know what happened to my friends?"

"They're in transit on one of the slow freighters. Safe for now, it's an out of the way, numbered system. I couldn't find out what kind of operation the Countess has going there. We can get to them."

"So you want to escape with me?" she asked excitedly.

"I'm absolutely terrified, I'm not too proud to admit it, but I can't stay here, not with her. Staying when I knew you were out there, alive, and devoting myself to the Countess and her companies was the hardest thing I've ever done. She has the largest slave trade in history, and I had to close some of the deals that made it grow. There are days when I can't stand myself. I haven't been able to find out what she's planning next, not specifically, but I know it was important to get you back, and to keep us together."

Aspen stroked his back. "We'll undo what we can, maybe steal some of what's hers for ourselves." The kiss that followed was slow, long and luscious.

"The Fleet Feather is always delivering and picking people up, it's our best chance. I get alerts whenever someone new lands, I'm the Countess's man for greeting new guests. I've been planning this for months, I even got a snapshot of the entire estate's database using General Grave's access codes."

"God, you're going to make an amazing criminal," she said, pressing against him for a moment before turning around. She kissed him over her shoulder as she guided his hands to her stomach.

"Why does that sound so exciting? "he returned her kiss as she moved his hands down slowly. "I like you more this way, curvy," he said between kisses. "Wild." His touch echoed his appreciation, following her form down over her hips, then slowly upward.

The shower door was flung open, and a quick, strong hand yanked her out by the arm. "None of that, you brats," she heard Master Kort grunt as he dragged her from the bathroom. His unnaturally broad features exaggerated his grimace as he dragged her through the next room then out into the hall. "What's this on you? Disgusting slob!"

She knew he was talking about the dye that had come loose from her skin, but Aspen didn't bother explaining. Her worry over what might happen next was the only thing on her mind. "Let me go!"

"And a slut," he said, shoving her through a bedroom door across the hall. Aspen stumbled and fell at the foot of a massive bed. "I may not have found you before the UCA, but that doesn't mean I'm going to let you ruin the Countess's plans for you now that you're here. You see these guards?" he said, gesturing to the armoured pair standing at her doorway. "You're on their leash now. Like their little fat dog. They will tell you where you have to go and when, what you have to do and with whom. They report directly to me, and if you misbehave in any way, I will punish you. It will be savage, and it will be public. Now wash yourself, and get six hours of sleep."

Aspen scowled at the door for long minutes after Master Kort was gone and it was closed. She was completely aware that, out of most of the slaves in service to the Countess, her situation wasn't so bad, but being told what to do by a master had her raging inside. Aware that anyone could be watching, she got up and made her way to the shower. It was identical to the one in Larken's room. It activated as soon as she was inside and she stood there for several minutes, letting the vibrating water spray do the work as Aspen took stock of everything she knew.

What she experienced with Larken, the change in him while they were alone, and how he seemed more like himself proved that he was worth trusting. Even though the encounter was cut short, Aspen found herself convinced that he was the person she remembered, but grown into a man she loved. It could all be a trick, the possibility couldn't be discounted, but the urge to trust him was powerful.

Even though he was only across the hallway, Aspen never missed Larken more, the ache she felt for him was as surprising as it was overwhelming. "Get yourself together," she said to herself as she watched the last of the green, yellow and brown ink slink down the drain between her feet. The shower deactivated and the drying cycle started. The walls reflected an image of her that was in conflict with what she thought she ought to look like. Blonde hair, tanned skin, and a face that still bore too much colour shifting, an alternative to makeup that could last forever. Her face was adorned with bronze and light rouge, it looked garish and wrong to her.

Once she was dry, she walked to the bed and fell in. The orders were clear, she was to have six hours of sleep and she knew there was only one way to get it. Aspen's frustration combined with her hunger pangs and thoughts of her crew would keep her up for days, unless she cheated. After wrapping herself in the thick comforter, she looked around the room one last time. The bed felt huge, and too soft compared to what she had become accustomed to on starships. The dimly lit room didn't feel safe, Aspen didn't have the power to determine who could come in and when, or even to lock the door. There was nothing she could do about it that night, and it was sure that she would be punished if she didn't do exactly as Master Kort ordered. Aspen gave her orders to the built in sleep assist. "Six hours, sounds sleep, wake me if anyone or anything enters."

The sensation of soothing waves, heat and massage comfort systems overtook her in minutes, and Aspen slipped into a deep, dreamless sleep.

05

The morning light stung Aspen's eyes as she rolled out of the blanket cocoon she spent the night in. The results of resting in a Rest maker bed never agreed with her, it always felt like there were extra cobwebs to shake. There was a thin, white dressing gown on the end of the bed, and she left it there on the way to the shower. There was no worry about anyone looking in through the windows, she could see nothing but blue ocean and sky. Even still, she was never shy, dolls didn't get permission to be.

Aspen emerged from the shower famished. "Good morning," said Tinick in a high, sing-song voice from the bedroom. Pieces of clothing were already laid out along the bottom of the bed, but what drew Aspen's attention immediately was a plate of food on a side table with two tall glasses of thick fruit juice and a tumbler of tea.

Tinick took her hands and led her to the table. "Eat everything, I'll make sure you're not disturbed, but I'll have to dress you at the same time." A napkin was pressed into Aspen's hand along with a large slice of pineapple. "You must be famished, so just dig in."

Aspen savoured the large slice of pineapple, something she hadn't tasted since she escaped. Even though it was a little difficult at first, she ate with a measured pace.

Tinick took her robe off while she was eating. Before she finished the second pineapple ring the tall, furred fashion master was pulling a light, transparent garment around Aspen that stretched from the middle of her ribs to below her hips. "The Countess wants you in this gown almost two weeks ahead of schedule, and she wants me to do my best to have you down to the size you are supposed to be then, only now." Tinick looked her in the eye and sighed. "If you ask me, you're a lovely young thing, there are so many things I could drape over your form and you'd look wonderful, but you know how this goes."

"The Countess gets what the Countess wants," Aspen said, realizing what was about to happen after glancing at the slim purple gown on the bed. She put the napkin down and finished swallowing her last bite of pineapple. "I'm glad you didn't let me finish that plate before this."

"Are you ready?" Tinick asked.

"How many sizes am I supposed to go down?"

"Three. Well, three and a bit," she said, activating the garment wrapped around her subject.

Aspen exhaled as most of her body was squeezed, almost falling over before it was finished. Then she tried to inhale and only caught a short breath. "Oh my God," she gasped. "To tight!"

Tinick loosened the garment's grip on her a little and Aspen was able to get most of a breath. "I've caught people," she gasped, "wearing these, is it always this tight?"

"Oh, you'd be surprised at how tight this could go before you actually passed out," Tinick said. "I hope you never find out for yourself, though. At least you're not risking cracked ribs or spinal deformity, I've seen both many times when someone is trying to fit into an outfit. You'd think that would be at and end, but self-adjusting clothing just isn't fashionable, I suppose. Try to finish your breakfast while you get used to that."

Aspen finally caught a full breath. "This isn't worth it," she said, gesturing at the dress. "And I don't know how much of that I'm going to get down while I'm being wrung out in the middle."

"Just try, I had to trade the plate they put together for you for this one. There is a guest down the hall who is wondering why they are breakfasting on a melon wedge and a glass of juice. Just don't sit down for a while after you've finished. I'm sorry to say, standing up straight may be the only way you can keep it down."

Aspen did as she was told since she was still hungry anyway and was part way though her second slice of melon when she asked; "So, how is it here at the new palace?"

"I've been busy," Tinick said. "There are many guests here who are wealthy refugees, so I've had to help dress most of them. The fashion industry has been just about crushed, since most manufacturing was driven by computers and machines. I've become important again," she said with a grin. "You never see them, but I have eight apprentices that are always sewing."

"I never considered how busy you'd be without AI's running the show."

"Oh yes, a transport leaves every week with the clothing I make for the houses that still have estates away from here. It left just yesterday, should be back next week for another shipment. The Countess has been generous enough to let me run my shop from here, but then, it's only a way to ensure that one of the last high calibre designers remains in her service."

Aspen made a mental note to watch for that shuttle, it didn't seem like the kind of thing that would be under heavy guard. She didn't like how long it would be before it would return, however. "Are there a lot of side businesses running on the property?"

"Keep eating," Tinick said before replying. "There are a number of them, all small operations though, so they use fast ships much like the Fleet Feather, only not quite as pretty."

Aspen carefully started on the pre-cut grape fruit. "Is there any trade with people on the planet?"

"Oh, no. This world is in recovery. It was one of the first places that the UCA carpet bombed, mostly with EMP's, when they started their campaign. The Countess moved in here shortly after her recovery, it didn't take much work to restore, and the shield blocks out everything she doesn't want to see. The Fleet Feather is our ferry. It's used so much that it's almost never locked when it touches down because there's always a pilot inside, I suppose. Every time I've been on it there's someone going here or there, mostly to the carrier hovering over the Countess's hemisphere." Tinick pointed out the window very specifically. "As soon as you leave the shield you can see it, a beautiful ship despite its purpose."

"What does it do up there?"

"It keeps everyone outside the shield surrounding the estate in line, of course."

"Of course."

"All right, let's get a few strawberries in you then get this dress on." She waited until Aspen ate the five strawberries on the plate, had a chance to wash her hands, then the long dark purple gown was pulled down onto her. There was some firm pulling and twisting involved in getting it to fit, but both of them were pleased with the results once the silky, long dress was fitted, though Aspen appreciated it begrudgingly. She could barely breathe, she had to take much shorter steps, and there was no doubt that she would be singled out once she attended whatever event was waiting for her that day. "What is this for?" she asked.

"Court is being held all day today. The Countess is making an announcement this morning, there is a luncheon this afternoon, then she is holding a celebration for the return of her Consort. He's conquered some new territory on a moon a few systems over, I couldn't be bothered to listen to the details, to be honest."

A knock on the door made Tinick jump a little. With a few long strides, she crossed the room, opened it and nearly growled; "A few minutes, please. She'll be out when she's ready."

The designer closed the door firmly and returned her attention to Aspen, straightening the neckline and pulling on the dress on her hips. "If I were to size this for you without the compression girdle, you'd look much better, but we all have our orders. This is for you," she said as she handed Aspen a small matching clutch. "The control for the girdle is inside."

Aspen was alarmed as a rectangular square with the word; INITIALIZING blinked along her outer forearm and Tinick didn't miss a beat as she wrapped one hand around the display, and held Aspen's hand with her other larger digits in a sweet gesture. "Do take care of yourself, I'll make sure there are a variety of properly fitted garments waiting for you when you come back. Oh, and take care with how you walk in this dress. The slits up the shins can rip all the way to the waist if you trip. The stitching is pretty, but not very strong."

Aspen smiled at Tinick, mentally ordering her computer to deactivate. "I'll be careful, thank you so much."

"Time to go," the woman said, gently guiding her to the door. "Remember, no rushing until you have to."

"I will," Aspen said, wondering what was able to reactivate her personal computer. It had to be something in the clutch, it only happened when Tinick put it in her hand, and the designer reacted to the screen on her skin activating so fast that she had to ask if she knew what was about to happen.

The computer and display were off by the time Tinick left her in the hallway, handing her off to Larken, who smiled warmly at her. "You look fantastic."

"Thank you. I can't breathe," Aspen said.

"Oh, the dress? I was talking about this," he said, caressing her cheek. "I didn't even notice the dress."

For a moment she forgot that there were four guards in platinum and gold armour behind them, that she was trying to plan an escape, and kissed him briefly.

"On we go, love birds," one of the guards said behind them. His voice was muffled by a round golden faceplate with platinum leaf embellishments. He looked ridiculous.

They were led to the main hall. It was empty this time except for a garish ornament in the centre with green and silver vines climbing a latticework that reached all the way to the ceiling. There was a place for two people to stand at the bottom, and the guards led them to it. "Do you have any idea why we're the centre piece this morning?" Aspen asked as courtiers trickled in.

"I don't know anything about this," Larken said as he took her hand. Her computer sent a passive notification that it just downloaded everything he had in his personal data storage the moment their hands touched. It was running exactly as she was accustomed. Most of the crewmembers of the Cool Angel had a program installed on their computers that could passively download the contents of systems it came into contact with. Aspen's could send simple notifications through her nervous system so she could see what it was doing, even when it was technically off. The display, sound and active systems were off, making it seem like there was no activity.

"I'm sorry about what happened last night," Larken whispered to her.

"That wasn't your fault," she replied.

"I could have taken a second to warn you instead of asking you questions and trying to explain myself."

"I mostly remember how good it felt to be with you," Aspen said, as much to reassure him as to make sure he knew she enjoyed their short private time together.

"Did you sleep?"

"I had to use the Dreamwave," Aspen replied. "I got some."

The Countess entered through the main doors then. Her dress was a loud affair with shifting rose, green and blue tints. The sleeves and the bottom were designed to look like outrageously large rose blooms that were only outdone by the one at the neckline that provided great panels behind her long neck and head. Aspen couldn't help but notice how frail she looked with her elongated arms, legs, neck and torso.

Courtiers applauded, some of whom were still coming in through doors hidden in the alcoves along the sides of the massive hall. It took at least half an hour for the hall to fill with murmuring, expectant courtiers, and when it did the sound of the main doors shutting echoed throughout the space.

The Countess' Consort emerged from the passage behind her throne. His dark purple jacket was adorned with silvered armour plates, and heavy tails along the back and sides moved with his stride as they struck his gold coloured, thick leggings.

His widened face grinned at the hundreds of courtiers before he gently took his lady's hand and kissed the back. Aspen wondered if he'd had more cybernetic and cosmetic work done in her absence. When she left he already had a full exoskeleton frame installed along with a secondary organ package that could take over if anything vital was destroyed. As for cosmetics, she knew his chest was broadened, legs lengthened and widened, and his face – a palette for only exaggerated expressions – looked broader than any human's should at the cheekbones and forehead. The Countess and her consort reminded her of creatures out of some fever induced nightmare where the laws of proportion were discarded in favour of horrifically twisted aesthetics that could only be distressing.

Kort stood beside the throne, grinning like some Cheshire creature, the metal irises in his eyes catching and reflecting light unnaturally. "Today my Countess will announce the impending arrival of a modern miracle. I call your attention to my radiant love, the one and only Countess of the Lucent Sector."

"Thank you," the Countess said. "My consort deserves a great deal of credit. He has hunted in the most dangerous parts of our space for the clues that will bring this idea to life. His dedication to this endeavour has endeared him to me even more. Cast your eyes to the middle of the room, you will see two beautiful creatures, my Larken and Aspen."

Aspen hated being on display for these people. They turned and practically leered at her. If she weren't so afraid of what the Countess was going to say next, she'd have found a way to excuse herself the moment eyes were back on the throne.

"They were made to match each other like perfect lovers before they were conceived. An amazing genesis centre in the Geist System fabricated a sperm and egg for each from scratch, then they were combined, and some time later, Aspen and Larken were born. Maturation and organic programming technology grew them until they were old enough, and well trained enough to be effective children to my court. This only took three months, there is no better technology anywhere else for creating perfect beings. Well, almost perfect. These enterprising scientists and business people knew that if they made my adopted children perfect, then I would have little reason to buy a new generation. They built in a feature that will end their lives in two years, and another that renders them unable to breed with each other or anyone else. Oh, they can try, and I was assured that the experience for them would be pleasurable, and that onlookers would be entertained, but there would be no offspring. I was willing to trade these limitations for the pair of angels you see before you now. Then things changed. The facilities they used were overrun by artificial intelligence controlled machines who slaughtered almost all of them. No one can order a perfect pair like these or any other variation. That is not where the story ends, however," the Countess said, gesturing to Kort.

He addressed the audience proudly. "I hunted down eleven people from the same facility that created these two. They managed to escape on their own, and almost all of them fell into service with criminal organizations or our competition. When they discovered that I was after them, their patrons tried to hide them, one of them tried to run, but they couldn't get away from me. Now we employ more experts from that facility than anyone. Only three of the skilled workers who know how Larken and his mate were made are in the wild, and I can assure you that they will be employed by us soon. The next step is to return to the Geist system and take the facilities that make such wonderful beings. We will go, and hold the site for as long as it takes. While we begin more important work, I will volunteer my own material so thousands of soldiers can be made to defend the planet. The first batch will be a pre-trained army for defence, after that, we will be able to sell you perfectly loyal, high-performing soldiers for your own armies. We have discovered that an adult human can be grown and programmed in these facilities in only seven months, not ten at a time, not a hundred at a time or a thousand, but ten thousand at a time." There was a smattering of applause, mostly from the United Core Authority officers, but from some household masters as well.

"Those are mere tools, and while they are certainty useful, they are not as impressive as our specimens here,"

The Countess said, gesturing towards Larken and Aspen. "When we arrive, Larken and Aspen will be analysed and the genetic locks that kept us from correcting their life expectancy limitations as well as their inability to breed will be cured. I will keep the first children they produce for myself, and they will be matured in the same facility that made the originals, so I can enjoy them as older children and watch them become as formidable as their parents." There were gasps of wonder and disbelief. Aspen felt a chill run down her spine as she realized that most of the courtiers were excited about her children being slaves the moment they were born. She always wanted to have a child, was haunted by the fact that it was impossible, but the implications had her head spinning. "The next generation, five babies seem to be Aspen's theoretical limit, will be perfect, natural children produced by their beautiful parents, and they will be auctioned off on their first birthday to you. You are all my very best friends, so this treasured generation will only be available to you." She was grinning, practically beaming, and the court was applauding, cheering so hard that it hurt her eardrums.

"It is every woman's dream to have children of their own, and I am looking forward to seeing Aspen become a mother, and for you all to share in the joy. I love her like my own though, so I will only allow her to have five pregnancies, then she and Larken will retire as treasured members of my court service. There is more, of course. My people will create new generations of perfect servants for you, as beautiful and as tailor made as my Larken and

Aspen. For a fee you can even determine their life expectancy, their intelligence level, base traits and whether or not they can be bred together. I know that even though you will be able to make generations of your own perfect little creatures, you'll return to the source for more, because I personally know the joy that Larken and Aspen have brought me."

Aspen could barely stop herself from shaking as she forced a smile and bowed with Larken. He was having difficulty containing himself as well, flushed red, and she squeezed his hands when they came together. "We have to celebrate this," she told him through clamped teeth.

His smile looked more like a grimace as he let his anger slip for a moment, but he nodded, and over the next few minutes they regained enough of their composure to stand together and smile at their Countess.

"Our forces, our estate here, and a force from the United Core Authority will be leaving for the Geist system in one week," Kort said. "I invite everyone here to come with us, and am happy to tell you that your participation will ensure a healthy discount when production begins. Now, celebrate! Today will mark the dawn of a new civilization!"

The rest of the day was a kind of hell Aspen could not have imagined. Everywhere she turned there was a courtier looking to congratulate her on her good fortune. They were eager to mention her extended life span, which she would have taken gladly, but many of them were even more interested in telling her how they would spare no expense in having the honour of buying one of her children for themselves. Aspen wanted to tear them apart, or to at least ask how they would feel if one of their children were sold to an owner who lived far away. Instead she grinned, and laughed along with them, accepting all their well-wishing.

All the while, she planned, taking fresh notice of where all those doors and the landing sites along the outskirts of the garden were.

06

Aspen refused to use the sleep assist technology in her bed that night, her trust in everything around her was absolutely gone. Thoughts of being breeding stock for years then who knew what plagued her along with other worries. Sun and her other friends could be stuck on some freighter, or already in a work camp.

When she did get to sleep she dreamt that she was a hooded guardian standing atop a tower that wobbled and bent in the wind. Faceless creatures swept in from a pitch black sky, picking at her, trying to pull her feet out from under her, and when she finally fell Aspen woke up violently, surging out of bed. The sun was coming up by the time she emerged from a hot shower.

Tinick was already at the foot of her bed with her wardrobe for the day and a steaming bowl of fried noodles and vegetables. "I love egg noodles, these are from a shop in the city that I prepare myself, I hope you like them." She said.

The aroma of the hot chicken, broccoli, carrot chunks in a salty citrus sauce wafted up to Aspen's nose and she couldn't help but smile. The long nosed nafalli grinned as she dug in with a pair of chopsticks. "Oh my God, this is not on my diet," she said around a mouthful of savoury noodles and chicken.

"Oh, the vegetables are, and the sauce is good for you, but you're right. I wouldn't go telling anyone you had this."

"You're going to get into trouble," Aspen said.

"Not when I force them to consider how many calories you'll be burning today. I'm afraid you're going to be entertaining the court in the garden and in the halls. Everyone has questions for you, my dear, everyone wants your attention. There are new shuttles arriving right now, in fact the Fleet Feather just landed with a whole delegation of people. The servants haven't even had time to unload their baggage. There's so much going on, I doubt anyone will bother me about slipping you some noodles and chicken, so eat up."

"Yes, Ma'am," Aspen replied, shovelling and slurping a load of noodles into her mouth.

"And step into these please," she said, holding a pair of black tights low for Aspen to step into. The next moment, she slipped a loose cap onto her head that dried, then styled her hair like a blonde wave that cascaded down her neck and shoulders but was drawn back from her face. "I don't know why we need cosmeticians about with these automatic stylers, but then again, they were saying the same thing about clothing designers only two years ago, so I should keep quiet I suppose," Tinick said as she took the empty bowl from Aspen and gave her a mask that was pre-set to do her makeup in bronze and black colours. Aspen looked at a mirror by the bed and was shocked at the result when the mask was finished applying the look. She almost didn't look like herself with the deep shadowy colours applied. The tunic was more understated than Aspen expected as well, open along the sides with broad bands that clung to the front, she looked slimmer than she actually was, for sure, but she was comfortable in bare arms and clingy matte tights.

"There, it's supposed to be hot today, so it's good that there are open spaces for your body to shed some of it, are you comfortable?"

"More than I have been since I arrived," Aspen said. "I don't know if the Countess will like it though."

"The colouring is right in fashion now, this is how everyone will be looking in a week, you watch," Tinick replied.

"Who am I to argue with an expert?"

"Larken is outside. He has been dressed to match. Perhaps I'll see you in the garden? I have permission to attend the Tai Chi session you'll be leading this morning."

"I can't believe I almost forgot to check my schedule," Aspen replied. Inwardly, the estate's duty schedule made her cringe. She enjoyed leading Yoga, Tai Chi, dance and poise classes for the guests before, but she felt like it was such a waste of time, considering what was going on. Aspen hoped that she didn't show her distaste openly. "Thank you so much for reminding me, I hope to see you there, Tinick."

The tall furred designer nodded and smiled as she left, leaving the door open for Larken, who was dressed in the same top and tights with copper highlights on his face. There were two guards behind him, one looked a bit like the one who gave her a meal bar on the day of her return, but Aspen couldn't be absolutely sure. "Hello Tinick, thank you for leaving everything out for me," he told her.

"My pleasure, try to have a good time today," Tinick replied as she moved down the hall. "Now I must attend the Countess and her party."

Larken let her go by and took Aspens hand as they headed into the hallway, their guards close behind. "Things are already starting, someone woke me up about half an hour ago. I was barely asleep anyway."

"What do you mean?" Aspen asked.

"The garden is full, the landing field is packed," Larken said. "Every major house in the system must have a representative here or on their way. Oh, I forgot to check." He stopped and tapped his forearm where a display appeared. "I hope she hasn't put it up on the public 'nets."

The Sellernet local to the solar system already had an advertisement up for new dolls, featuring clips of her and Larken growing up. They were adorable, even she had to admit as she watched them morph from children into young adults.

"You guys were so cute," one of the guards said. His partner nudged him with her elbow.

Aspen watched in horror as the display showed footage from their short shower together, only it didn't end with her getting unceremoniously yanked out by Kort, but went on as though they were never interrupted. They even added dialog. This fictional Larken and Aspen made declarations of love and devotion as they caressed each other. If it weren't on the public Stellarnet, she would only be mildly irritated, she wasn't a shy person and she wished things did happen as they were depicted in that hologram, but she was furious. "How could she do this?"

"You two are love birds, and she's trying to sell copies to bird watchers," the female guard whispered.

"How would you feel if you were going to be used as a breeding mare?" Aspen said, whirling on her.

"Don't," Larken said. "They can't do anything."

"Listen to him," the female guard agreed.

"No, I'm going to be popping babies out for at least five years and watching them get sent away. Then, when they're barely old enough, they might become breeding stock too, or get sold into a harem somewhere, or worse."

"It happens all the time to normal slaves, and there's nothing anyone can do," the male guard said. "Move on to the garden please."

Larken squeezed her hand and she allowed herself to be led to the garden. There was something about him, he didn't seem worried about the future, or insulted by the holo of them in the shower. There must have been something going on that she wasn't seeing, he must have a plan. Then she remembered, he'd already told her that he'd make sure they would be the welcoming committee for new shuttles, and there were so many arriving already.

The only thing that enticed Aspen to stay was the idea that she may have her life extended, the clock might stop ticking or at least slow down to a normal crawl. They stopped in the foyer where Kort joined them with two guards of his own. Their chitinous purple and gold armour looked weathered, more practical than what the guards wore in the estate. "I think I'll take escort duty for now. Are we going to the garden?" Kort said, smiling too closely and too broadly at her.

"I thought we'd greet newcomers as they arrived," Larken said.

"I don't think so. Security will be checking every shuttle that arrives, we can't put you or your mate at risk. In fact, we'll be putting you both in stasis later today so we can hide you aboard my carrier. Your value as a pair has gone up higher than we'd hoped."

The male guard who was at her door looked to Aspen and Larken. "Good luck, you two. I hope they fix you up."

Kort regarded him with a scowl. "They need help scanning the new guests in the garden platform, you're with us, but you're going to keep your mouths shut and your eyes open."

"Yes, Sir," the pair of them replied.

The walk to the garden platform was a silent one, with Kort walking close behind her and Larken, they were surrounded by the old and new guards. They passed the garish, trickling fountains. The sun felt hot on her face, and all the new arrivals seemed too cheerful for her liking. People she'd never met smiled at her expectantly as she passed, until one woman – her brown and violet hair was up in a circular hoop above her head that made her look ridiculous – ignored the guards and embraced Larken. "I was so disappointed when I didn't get to see you on my last visit, Larken!" she exclaimed. Aspen knew her, she was a long time courtier who didn't pay her much attention, but had great affection for Larken.

"Lady Gadanne, how are you?" Larken asked, feigning joy at seeing her. "I'm happy I could see you before we go." Aspen smiled at her and then turned her attention to the large marble ramp leading down to the grassy landing field. There were no guards nearby, they were occupied with the new arrivals, but the Fleet Feather was right where it aught to be at the bottom of the ramp, and the door was open.

"You're leaving so soon? I was so hoping we could sit, or walk the grounds for a while, especially now that you have your Aspen back. You seemed so forlorn while she was away. It's good to see you whole again. I don't know what I'd do if my new husband were to disappear," the Lady said.

Aspen stopped following the conversation as Kort's hand landed on her hip and slowly began to slip downwards. Larken was too distracted by Lady Gadanne to notice, and the guards knew not to do anything about it. "When he's in stasis, I'll wake you up so we can have some fun before you get fixed. I wonder, did you learn any new tricks while you were away? I know you lost your virginity while you were out there, it was on the scans," he whispered.

Aspen wished she could rip his hand off and stuff it in his mouth. Whether it was because of her rising anger, or just by chance, she didn't know, but her eye came to rest on the female guard that had come for her that morning. Specifically, she found herself staring at the woman's sidearm, which was resting in its holster without the safety latch engaged.

She snatched the handgun from where it hung, turned, started pulling on the trigger, found the safety with her other hand and struck Kort in the face and chest with half the white energy bolts the blaster fired. "Run!" Aspen said as the smell of burned flesh filled her nostrils and she burst into a run.

"Sorry!" Larken said to Lady Gadanne as he followed her.

Aspen dropped the handgun as she scrambled past a few guests, and didn't bother stopping.

Larken was beside her as she sprinted over an arched bridge that was built into one of the most grandiose fountains.

Several yellow bolts of energy passed through the air wide of them as they sprinted between the fountains. "They're shooting?" Larken asked, shocked.

"Stun shots! We have to keep going!"

They made it down to the landing spot then into the Fleet Feather. Aspen rushed up the stairs to the cockpit hatch before the pilot, an old, chubby man with a head of hair cut perfectly equal to a full beard, could close it.

He fished a handgun out from its holster somewhere between his legs and fired at her wildly, barely managing to half-turn while his pilot chair refused to cooperate. "Get off my ship!" he shouted, unable to hit her while his seat slowly turned. From behind his seat she slapped the gun out of his hand and avoided his grasp.

Aspen stuffed her fingers into the back of the collar of his containment suit and leaned back. The pilot frantically scrambled to pull the front of the collar loose as he fought for air. She pressed against the back of the seat with her knees as he struggled, trapping him against the seat and cutting off his air completely.

It was the hardest thing she'd ever done, listening to him choke, feeling the fight slip out of him as he passed into unconsciousness then finally dying. When she was sure he was dead, she let him go and watched the body slump in the pilot's seat.

His control panel was already active, unlocked and ready for the next group who wanted to be ferried around. "Close the hatch, Larken!"

She rushed to the controls and activated the emergency ascension, getting the navigational system to start calculating a jump from orbit. "I can't believe it, we're almost out of here." Ragged breathing was her answer.

"Larken?" she asked, turning around.

"Made it," he said, coughing wetly. "Inside and outside hatches are closed."

He was slumped down against the back wall, two holes the size of her fist through his middle and one in the middle of his chest. The handgun the pilot used was a shredder, it didn't hit hard enough to damage most electronics much, but it tore through flesh raggedly, savagely. "Oh, no," Aspen said, taking him into his arms. "I'm sorry, my love. I'm so sorry."

Her hand touched something soft with jagged pieces sticking out when she tried to cradle his head in it, and it came away covered in blood. He was bleeding profusely everywhere. Aspen's mind raced as she tried to find a way to save him. There were emergency kits aboard, but there was nothing that could help him there, and she knew for a fact that there were no automatic medical treatment systems aboard. If they were ever present, they were ripped out to make room for luxury cabins.

He reached up and caressed her face. "It's okay," he breathed, pain creasing his forehead. "We were together. I can't believe you got us out. I did okay? I didn't slow you down?"

"You were perfect," Aspen said, kissing his forehead and brushing his hair from his face. "Rest, just rest. There must be an emergency kit here, maybe something to slow this down." She started to get out from under him but he gripped her tunic. She let herself be dragged down to kiss him, and tasted blood on his lips.

He looked to the cockpit window and saw space. "I'm free," he said. "I'm free with you," he struggled with another breath.

"You're free," Aspen said. "I love you so much, Larken."

"Love you too, always loved you," he said. "Find someone who-" he struggled.

"Shh," she said, brushing her lips against his. She didn't want to be told to move on.

"-makes you laugh," he finished. "I always loved watching you laugh. And don't let her get you." He breathed. "I…" His chest quaked, his hand gripped hers hard, and he breathed rapidly, blood gurgling in his chest and sputtering through his lips. There was panic in his eyes.

"Larken, I love you, I'm so sorry I did this. I love you."

His eyes finally lost focus, he stopped breathing and he fell limp. Aspen stared at his face. This would be how she would remember him, she knew from experience. When the artificial intelligences took over and killed most of the people in the Countess's household she saw people she grew up with die, and no matter how wonderful those people were, she could only ever remember their faces as they were in the throes of panic or fear.

Larken would forever look like he was in pain and afraid. She wouldn't remember holding his hand in the garden when they were children, without recalling how he clutched hers as his body failed him. Memories of staring contests, and nose-to-nose closeness where they would look into each other's eyes would conjure up a memory of his dead gaze.

The navigational computer beeped, indicating that the emergency jump coordinates were calculated and the ship was in position. There were alerts on the combat scanner's screen – ships were coming to get them. Aspen slowly got to her feet, crossed to the console and confirmed that she wanted to make the jump and the ship began hyper-accelerating into a wormhole of its own creation.

Aspen checked all the security systems to make sure there was no one else aboard, cut power to the transponder and curled up in the back corner of the cockpit. "I got out," she whispered to herself. "But I left half of me behind." Not for the first time, Aspen wished her tear ducts would allow her to cry. Her sobs came anyway, so hard that her stomach and ribs hurt by the time she felt numb.

07

Spin slowly realized that she had to make sure she had full control of the ship, then get rid of the pilot. Half numb to the world around her, she went through the motions of adding herself into the system then crashing the security software, taking the seconds it took for it to restart to add herself as the new captain. If the main console weren't already unlocked, she wouldn't have been able to do it, but the pilot was busy getting the ship ready for take-off when she killed him.

"You're going to spin in space forever, asshole," she said to him as she turned the seat towards the door and pushed him face first onto the deck. "I'll have to write something on your forehead just in case someone finds you out there."

Looking past his corpse she saw Larken and a pang of sadness struck her. It was followed by something that burned just as deeply – anger. "I'm going to make every one of them suffer."

The console behind her beeped twice quickly, indicating that they were close to coming out of faster than light travel mode. Aspen set it to start calculating the next jump, a longer stretch that took the Fleet Feather to a charted world it had never been to before so she could lessen the chances of pursuers guessing her destination. Kort would be the first to come for her. He was legendary for cheating death, and she was sure the damage she did – though significant – wasn't enough to put him down.

Using her new Captain's access, she deactivated the transponder and entered her personal communication codes, so the ship wouldn't contact anyone using its own identity. Running with smugglers for a year had taught her many tricks.

Sadly, it didn't make getting rid of one body and figuring out what to do with another one that was much more treasured any easier. Aspen opened the armoured cockpit door and heard voices coming up from below. After closing and locking it quietly, she checked the internal security monitor and discovered that there were four lower members of the Countess's court from the Rinnel company sitting together. She recognized two of them right away – Tilly and Dexter Rinnel. They were children in a growing empire and professional lobbyists who were partially responsible for having laws against slavery repealed on dozens of civilized worlds, and that was before the Basic Era started. Aspen could only imagine how easy it must have been after artificial intelligences went mad and began to fight each other for them to do business as slavers. There were numerous worlds where the military destroyed all the complex technology with electromagnetic pulse bombs, leaving millions of people stranded.

As Aspen stared at them on the screen she wondered how many dolls their company owned, and how many they sold. It took her seconds to find the pilot's sidearm and check it for ammunition. He'd expended fourteen shots, there were twenty-one left. She found two more clips in the drawer in his console along with a few snack bars, a bag of dill rice puffs, a pair of women's underwear which she discarded without touching, and control chips for devices across the ship. "Thank God you were a stupid pervert. You may as well have left the whole ship unlocked."

She searched him rapidly, finding the data chip containing the ownership documents for the ship in his boot and another snack bar. The ship emerged from faster than light mode and Aspen checked the scans of the area. There was an unmanned communication station, and a slow transit shuttle at long range.

With a few button presses she set the computer to jump as soon as anything with a weapon arrived in the area. She had some cleaning to do before moving on.

Gun in hand, Aspen opened the hatch and walked down the stairs into the main passenger area.

"Oh my God, what happened, Aspen?" asked Tilly, her slender hand covering her mouth.

Spin almost forgot that she was covered in Larken's blood. "Stand up and get against that bulkhead," she said, raising the weapon and pointing it at Dexter Rinnel. "All of you."

"She's gone insane, I've heard of this happening to dolls," Tilly said, clutching his arm.

With nary a thought, Aspen fired at the seat next to one of the servants. The round burst apart in the air, sending spinning fragments forward in a shot seven centimetres wide. Her soft target exploded in a puff of white padding. "Do it! Now!" she shouted.

They rushed to the bulkhead, hands raised, shrinking away from her. "Where were you when the ship took off?"

"We were already settling into our quarters," Dexter explained. "We were the last to move our things in and were almost on our way off."

"You were going to make the journey to Geist aboard the Fleet Feather? Don't lie, I can check the manifest."

"Yes, we're out of favour with the Countess, so we don't get to travel with her."

That sounded right to Aspen. "Is there anyone else on the ship?"

"No, just personal luggage and a dog," Tilly replied, curling up against her brother's side.

"All right, "Aspen said. "There is a corpse up there; a fat man. I want your servants to drag it to the starboard airlock right there. Do you understand?"

"I understand." Dexter said, his arm around his sister. "We'll do anything you ask us to if you'll let us live."

"Order them to move the body, "Aspen said, carefully aiming the handgun at Tilly, who whimpered and covered her eyes.

Dexter nodded at his servants and the pair of them rushed up the stairs. "Is that Larken?" one of them asked, shocked.

"Leave him alone!" Aspen said, not taking her eyes off the the Rinnels leaning against the bulkhead across the cabin. "Just the fat one. Drag him."

They followed her orders and dragged him to the airlock face down. "Good, now put him in the airlock and get in there with him. Don't worry, it's safe, the airlock won't open while we're under way." Aspen said, using her best reassuring tone.

"Listen, I don't know what happened, and I'm sorry if Larken is hurt up there. Maybe we can help," Dexter offered.

"Do you have anything that can restore a human brain? Can you get it here in the next hour?"

Dexter was silent. Everyone there knew the answer already. Aspen glanced at the servants and nodded towards the airlock. "Get in, don't worry." She returned her focus to Dexter and his sister. "Order them to do it."

"I won't," one of the servants said, bursting into tears. "Not with him," she pointed at the corpse and wailed incoherently.

"Just push him into it and sit down beside the airlock, then," Aspen said. The wailing servant, lovely in her own right but near panic, reminded her not to spread her revenge too widely. They weren't responsible for anything, there was no need to space them with the pilot's corpse, especially since they pushed him into the airlock quickly, closing the inner doors behind him. They also didn't look like any generation of doll Aspen had ever seen, so they probably weren't brainwashed into serving their masters like many she'd known. The servants sat down as soon as they were finished, their backs against the bulkhead beside the airlock. "Thank you," Aspen said.

Spin looked back to Dexter then, all emotions but anger draining from her. She touched her wrist, starting a recording. "Now Dex, we've met before. You remember?"

"I do," he said. "A long time ago. We got along."

"No, I led you to think we were getting along. Sure, you were kind, but I could tell you were only trying to assess my value before making an offer to the Countess. That's what you and your sister do, you barter, you trade, and you grow your little empire for your family."

"You were too precious to her," Dexter said. "You should be proud."

"You came to the palace yesterday to see Larken and me, didn't you?"

"No, we heard there would be a big announcement, that our business would benefit, so we attended. I didn't regret it until now."

"I wonder, were you more interested in the new dolls from the New Skin Facility, or in buying my babies?" Aspen waited for a response, but Dexter was too smart to offer one and Tilly was terrified. "I want you to repeat after me: Transfer seventy-seven million UCA credits…"

"Transfer seventy-seven million UCA credits…" Dexter repeated.

"To the account number provided…"

Dexter's expression darkened as he repeated; "To the account number provided…"

"And the location of your children will be transmitted to you."

"I'm not doing this," Dexter said. "There's no way I'm going to get ransomed."

"All right," Aspen said, "then I'll record my own message." She cleared her throat. "If you do not transmit seventy-seven million UCA credits for each one of these captives to the account provided, you will never know the location of your children's bodies."

Tilly screeched and hid her face against her brother. For a grown woman, she did a good impression of a frightened little girl. "All right!" Dexter said. "You will receive the location of your children when the money is received!" he shouted. "Good enough?"

"Good, get in the hyper-pod, now."

Dexter opened the round, red and white hatch and helped his sister into the escape pod. "You're going to pay for this, there is no doubt, and we won't take money as reparation." He growled.

"Get in the pod!" Aspen shrieked, taking several steps forward with the gun levelled at his head. Startled, he fell inside, tangling with his sister and her frilly yellow dress.

Spin slammed the inner hatch shut, followed by the outer hatch and locked it. She edited and transmitted the ransom demand without launching the pod. It wasn't the place, the area was too busy, it was too close to the Countess' estate. With the message sent, she used a small access console and her new Captain's code to initiate the Fleet Feather's next faster than light jump.

"What about us?" asked the braver of the two servants. She had nice, big brown eyes and long strawberry blonde hair.

"You're both slaves?" Aspen asked.

"We were both taken from Starfall City, that's how we met," she replied.

"Do you want to be free?"

The weeping one raised her head and nodded.

"Of course, I don't know where to go, and we don't have any money, but yes."

"Then you're free," Aspen said. "And I'll give you each one million credits when their family pays me."

The weeping servant stroked brown hair out of her eyes, wiped her tears away and got to her feet. "Don't shoot, I have something I've wanted to do for a while."

Spin shrugged and kept the gun at her side as she watched the servant stride to the small porthole looking into the escape pod and spat with vigour then made several rude gestures. It almost looked like a dance, a fairly well practiced one. She turned away from her former masters with a satisfied smile. "Thank you, that felt really good."

"Listen," the other one said, standing slowly. "I know you don't trust us, you shouldn't, but it looks like you've had a really rough time. I'd like to help."

"I don't know how you could," Aspen said, lowering her head.

"I'm Mirra, and she's Della," the strawberry blonde one said. Set whatever security is on this ship to watch us, keep us from transmitting out or whatever, and we'll get you cleaned up. I know I can find some clothes in one of the guest quarters, so we'll get you changed. Let us take care of you. Maybe earn that fresh start you're setting us up with. I know you've run before, everyone does, so I believe you'll help us get away."

Della smiled at her and touched her arm gently. "Let us help you, okay?"

Spin didn't turn the gun's safety on because she trusted them. It was weariness that led her to accept their offer. "Okay, just give me a minute." There was a list of things to do building in her head, all the things she needed to do before she attempted to rescue Sun and the rest of her people. The first thing on it was to make the ship safe.

Mirra and Della followed her up to the cockpit, where Della immediately stopped and whispered; "I'm going to get a sheet, okay?"

Spin set the ship security system to track her and Mirra's movements then nodded. Before she was finished scanning the rest of the ship for more passengers, Della returned with a sheet and gently laid it on Larken's body. "I always liked him, such a nice man. He had a little smile for me every time he caught me staring at him. Asked me how I was once, and I think he listened when I answered."

Spin swallowed her grief and shook her head as the scan completed. There was one small life form aboard in a stasis cube, it was checked in as a Pomeranian. "Someone brought a dog." She said.

"Oh, that's Lady Friss' pup," Della said.

"You could probably ransom that too," Mirra added. "I'm sure she'd pay five million, maybe a lot more, that dog is like her only child."

"I'll give it a try, it'll keep for months in its stasis cube," Aspen said, her mouth was running on autopilot. They arrived at their new destination, emerging from faster than light travel. "Time to send coordinates out and your masters into space." That, she said with great pleasure, pointing at a switch with a safety cover on the right hand side of the large cockpit. "Who wants the honours?"

"I'll open the cover, you flick the switch," Mirra said, smiling at Della.

Della hopped and giggled giddily. "Do it!"

Spin started setting up their next jump, a much longer course that took them past several systems before arriving at a quiet backwater the Cool Angel used to take on supplies often. Mirra flipped the cover up, and Della flicked the switch with an exaggerated gesture.

A thud echoed from below, and the scanners confirmed that the pod was away with two live passengers. Aspen turned the ship so their servants could see it disappear into the distance through the transparent metal canopy. With a few button presses the course was recorded so it could be sent to their family if they paid the ransom.

"Wave bye-bye," Della said. "Thank you so much for this, Aspen. I can't believe we'll never have to look after those rich assholes again."

The navigational system chirped, indicating that it was finished plotting. Aspen checked the course and set it to make the next jump. The three of them were silent as the ship turned and slipped into another wormhole. "Let's get you cleaned up." Mirra said in a gentle tone.

They led her to the nicest guest shower, a stall Aspen had seen before, but was never allowed to use, and undressed her tenderly. "I'm going to go find some clothes," Della said. "What do you want?"

"If you find an under suit, that'd be the best thing."

"Like a spacer's containment suit?" Della asked, holding her hands wide around her hips and torso, miming a large exploration suit.

"She means the ones that conform so you can wear clothes over them, there should be one near crew quarters by the engine room," Mirra said.

"Oh, I like those, the better ones, anyway."

"Check medication, too if you can," Aspen said. "You're looking for anything that begins with Nacro or Cetri."

"Those are mind altering," Mirra said, taking her dress off. "Powerful."

"I need to clear my head a little," Aspen said, about to ask what she was doing when Mirra gently put her in the warm spray of the shower and wet a washcloth, following her in. "I can wash myself."

"There's nothing more relaxing than letting someone take care of you. I've been doing this for years, trust me," she replied with a gentle smile.

Spin peeked at the spot her computer display was tattooed on her arm, and it showed her – and only her – an image of Della running towards empty crew quarters. With her nod of permission, Mirra began washing the blood off her, and she closed her eyes.

Her touch was firm but soothing, what she thought a mother's touch must be like.

"All finished," Mirra said as Aspen was just starting to relax to the point where she thought she could slip into a snooze. "Out, before we get prune-y."

"You look all clean and new," Della said as she dropped an armful of clothing and other things onto the bed. "I found these," she said, presenting her with a slim bottle of pills.

Spin looked at the name then the stamp on the top pill and nodded. "It's strong enough, but I won't lose any memories permanently," she said, popping one in and crunching it. It was so bitter she flinched.

"You okay?" Della asked.

"Just shouldn't have bitten that one," Aspen said, already feeling the emotions surrounding Larken's death fading, her love for him was going with it, and she was glad it wasn't permanent.

"How does it work?" Mirra asked, pulling a blue and white jumpsuit from the pile of clothing and sizing it up.

Spin sighed, her head clearing. "Agoes, or Cetrimemodel helps the mind locate traumatic memory and then turns the volume down on them, so I can process them slowly. It doesn't mess with long term memory, so I won't lose anything. These last thirty standard days per pill, they're the expensive ones. Really expensive, I could get five thousand credits apiece for them."

"That I knew," Della said. "Tilly doesn't take anything but these, and she takes them a lot, like two every three days? That can't be right…"

"No, you can abuse 'em, they'll start flipping switches in your brain, turning depressing thoughts into the funniest thing, but it stops working on fear and anxiety before long."

"That really explains a lot," Della said. "This is what I could find after going through about half the cabins." She gestured to the bed where she'd laid dozens of articles of clothing in a pile. "It's all clean, I don't know what you want to look like though. I got a few things for Mirra and me too, hope that's okay. I don't want to wear this stupid maid outfit a moment longer than I have to."

Aspen nodded. "They're a bit conspicuous. Go ahead and change." She laughed at how quickly the maids' uniforms came off. Della stripped faster than her counterpart, and with a celebratory flair. "You're enjoying this way too much."

"Ripping these off and getting into the closets of our masters? You betcha," she replied, holding up a thin, white containment suit that sealed up the front. "This would look good on you, but it's not an undersuit. The tag says it's a Class V Containment Suit, whatever that means, but I don't think it would fit under anything tight," she said. "I didn't know if you'd want it."

Spin took it and admired the smooth, stretchy fabric. Her computer linked with it and extended the range of its sensors, picking up multiple built in devices. "I think you already know me, Della," she said, opening it and slipping it on with her help. A display on the thigh asked her what colour she wanted it to be and she pondered.

"You always looked good in purple," Della said, and Mirra elbowed her.

"That's her master's house colour."

"Oh, then not purple, sorry."

"It's okay," Aspen said. She was sure that if she wasn't medicated she would have been irritated, but that emotion seemed so far away. "I've always liked blue skies, and water." The suit changed to sky blue then fitted to her shape comfortably. "I wore a consuit for over a year, but not one this well made."

"A containment suit for the rich," Mirra said.

"You're right, it was from Lady Supta's cabin, not the crew quarters. What I found there was pretty boring compared to this, and they said they were Class E anyway. Class V is better?"

"Class V is better," Aspen said, nodding and flexing her fingers. The gloves conformed to her digits perfectly. "Thank you."

"Tell me you found something for her to put on over it?" Mirra said, putting her similar suit on. She finished shimmying her shoulders into her own suit then activated it. "Unless you like showing off, drawing a little attention."

"Not on most days." Aspen had seen spacers wearing much tighter, more revealing suits, but she admitted she'd rather have more. Besides, there was only a small pocket on her hip for storage, not nearly enough.

"I knew that would be a problem," Della said. "I have this white jacket, a heavy black one, and a black chromatic one with buckles down the front."

"Do any of them have armour built in?" Aspen asked, taking the chromatic jacket from Della. The heavy cloth base felt like it was rubberized, and it was jet black beneath the chromium treatment, which was a layer of colour that shifted as it moved. The label said ray refracting coating had been applied.

"Well, no, none of the jackets I did had an armour rating tag. I only checked a few places though."

Spin held the jacket up to the light. "That's okay, I think this looks right for me, and I've seen this treatment before," she said. "Some mercenaries add it to their armour so they're pretty much stun-proof and energy weapons aren't as effective. She put it on and liked the significant weight it put on her shoulders, the cloth was so heavy it felt like she was being held. Another tag on the inside boasted that there were more layers available for installation and she hoped she could find a place that still had them.

"It looks good on you," Mirra said.

"Okay, now I laughed when I saw these too, but give it a minute," Della said, reaching down beside the bed. She yanked up a pair of black thigh-high boots with thin, black armour plates along the front. Aspen laughed at them as soon as she saw them, shaking her head. "No way!"

Mirra laughed as well, crossing the room and touching them, looking like an entirely different person in her fitted, glossy green jumpsuit. "Oh, no, you have to wear these," she said. "You're a kick-ass lady, and these are a kick-ass lady's boots."

"How do you even put those on? It looks like they stand on their own," she laughed.

Mirra pushed her onto the bed and said; "You lay down."

Della handed the right one to Aspen, who pulled it up over the leg of her containment suit. As soon as her foot was planted all the way inside, the boot conformed to her leg, shortening so the top ended in the middle of her thigh and hugged the rest of her leg. Her foot felt snugly planted, as though the boot was already broken in just right. Without a word, she pulled the other one on and smiled as she got to her feet. "They feel too nice."

"There are extra straps here for something," Della said, tugging at the inside of the top of her boot.

Spin looked at them and realized what they were for. "You can strap a gun holster or tool pocket to the outside of each boot."

"You've gotta keep them now," Mirra said, pulling her in front of the mirror. "You look way too badass."

Della ran her hand down the front of Aspen's consuit until it was open down to the naval. "Better."

Spin blushed and closed it back up until it was still open a little, but modestly. "There."

"What are your plans for the ship?" Mirra asked.

"I don't know if I'm keeping it," Aspen said. She was thankful her head was clear. Trusting them aboard was a risk she started taking when she was still half out of her mind. Trusting them with more information than she had to was another kind of trust entirely. "The Fleet Feather is so conspicuous, I don't think I could go anywhere in the sector without being recognized. Why do you ask?"

"I've been a ship hand before," Mirra said. "And I did time in a galley on an old cargo hauler. I mean, I can't fix your reactor, but I know how to turn a wrench, and I'll be running for a while anyway. That, and I was wondering if we're dressing you for a tea party – in which case we have to start over – or if you're planning to do more, ahem, business. I mean, you took to kidnapping like a fish to water."

"I've seen a few from the other end," Aspen explained.

"I'd sign up for this ship," Della added. "Even if you just need someone to keep it clean."

"We'll see if I still have a ship in a few days," Aspen said. "But you're right, there's more business coming. I think I'm dressed for it."

Della handed her the pilot's gun, she'd found the holster and put the two together. There was a strap with six clips in it. Aspen hadn't even realized that she'd lost track of her weapon. "You're going to need this. I wish I was good in a fight, or could fly a ship, or even shoot a gun, but I'm pretty useless when you look at it. I can clean though, and take care of people."

"That's the kind of thing that makes a ship feel like a home," Aspen said, trying to adjust the straps at the top of her boot so they made loops that would hold clips along the front. Mirra helped, providing the third hand she was missing. "She can cook like a gourmet droid, make something out of three pieces of nothing."

"Shush, you'll raise expectations," Della said as she took Aspen's jacket and found the right way to hang the gun holster inside it. "I promise I'll never give you a reason to point that at me again," she said as she put the jacket back on Aspen. The gun wasn't so weighty that it felt off balance, and it only took her a moment to adjust to it hanging under her shoulder. She faintly wished she had something else, a weapon that didn't kill the person she loved more than anything in the universe, but it was an intimidating weapon.

"I really hope that's true," Aspen said. "But you may be safer going off on your own after you get paid. This ship is already wanted, and I'm positive that I'm headed into another dangerous situation. Just think about it, I appreciate your offer to help, and if I end up with a ship to call my own at the end of this, I'll need people just like you, but the danger is very real. I don't want you to follow me into something you can't handle because you thought you owed me." She recalled a moment where she considered spacing them and felt a dull pang of guilt. "You would have ended up with a head start one way or another. How you decide to use your freedom is up to you, and I'd love it if you joined me on a ship, but it probably won't be this one, and I know I'm dangerous to be around. They enslave or execute outlaws here, and that's what I am now."

"We know," Della said. "For the right reasons."

"What she said," Mirra added. "Now let's see what else we can find aboard."

"We split platinum so I get seventy percent, you two split the rest," Aspen said.

"What? But..." Della said.

"That's how captains do it," Mirra said. "Most actually take between eighty or ninety-five, because of the cost of maintaining the ship and the responsibility they shoulder."

"Oh, that makes sense."

"Besides, we're going to find a lot of plat," Mirra said. "There was a lot of heavy luggage delivered ahead of us."

"We should start piling valuables and staples in the main hold too," Aspen said. "We need to know how much loose items of value and food we have. The galley is always stocked on this old bird before long trips, so I'll check that with a quick look."

"Can I go clothes hunting while we do this?" Della asked.

"Sure," Aspen said. "We're on an eleven-hour jump, then at least one more after that. I'm just hoping the Rinnel family pays up. I only have three thousand credits in my personal account. I can't cover your shares from the ransom attempt on that."

"I haven't been allowed to have a bank account for seven years," Della said.

"What she said," Mirra added.

"Okay, you two get started, I'm going to plan our next jump," said.

So the looting began while Aspen made sure the galley was stocked and was satisfied that every cupboard and dispenser was full, then returned to the cockpit, averting her eyes from the sheet against the rear bulkhead.

It only took her a few minutes to find where Sun and the three other crewmembers were brought, and it wasn't where she'd hoped. They were working in a fungus yard on Tullast, skimming food from a swampy plantation as it rose to the surface – if you could call that protein scum food.

She'd visited the prettier sides of Tullast with the Countess when she and Larken were young teenagers. The beaches and springs there were beautiful, and they had a lot of carefree time while the Countess attended to other business.

Spin returned to the matter at hand. The rescue was problematic. The ground was soft, so she'd have to carefully hover so people could get on, but she wouldn't know where her friends were until she got within ten kilometres so she could scan for their biometrics readings.

A hard scan like that would raise suspicion, so she needed someone to make some noise. The only thing she could think of was putting Della and Mirra in two of the five gun turrets and using one of the forward missile launchers to blow something up. It was risky, she had no idea if either of them could shoot, and would risk setting a processing tank off if she fired a missile anywhere but the swampy open fungus pit, and that's where her friends would most likely be.

The plan looked ugly no matter how she approached it. She wished she could just set the Fleet Feather down and pretend she was about the Countess' business, but there was a fair chance that someone sent a message to Tullast, telling the foremen there to expect a breakout attempt.

She left the cockpit and made her way to the rear hold, deciding on a plan by the time she got there. "Okay, I'm going to need your help to pull this off." She said, then stopped at the sight of racks of clothing, cases of fine bottles with even finer liquids inside, and three metal bullion cases.

"These are full," Della said, tossing a glittering rectangle of platinum at her. It glittered in her hand, the serial number and UCA stamped along with the denomination – 1,000 – in industrial grade blue diamonds. "Fifty thousand molecularly stamped platinum in each case in large denominations. That piece isn't from the cases."

"It's from some of the loose plat we found, about seventeen thousand worth from the luggage. There's also another twenty-eight thousand from our old master's personal safe," Mirra said, smiling as much as Della.

"You guys keep that," said, in awe of the cash they'd found and how organized everything else was. "We'll split the cased and loose stuff the way we discussed if that's all right."

"You're going to have to stop asking us if it's all right," Della said. "If you're going to be a captain."

"I'm not a captain, I've pirated a ship and technically stolen two slaves that I'll be setting free. I'm an escaped slave whose devalued because her mated partner is dead, and an outlaw for theft and kidnapping. When someone checks the Stellarnet for the definition of 'trouble' in the future, there will be a picture of me."

"We're going to be hard to get rid of," Mirra said. "If this is the kind of trouble you get into, I think I want to get involved, at least for a while."

"We'll see." Aspen ran her hands down one of the clothing racks and shook her head. "You did this in the hour I was in the cockpit. I can't believe it. I also expected to find a mountain of clothing and other loot just dumped in the cargo bay, that's how most quick looting jobs go."

"We're better at quickies, I guess," Della said.

"So, where are we going to sell our booty?" Mirra asked.

"Well, we're going to get ready to take on some passengers' tomorrow, so we'll have to lock it up once you two are finished taking your pick of clothes. Then, well, I know a few places that should buy most of this stuff.

Maybe, it's dangerous. We're going to have bounties on our heads, slave hunters might already be looking for us. Anyway, dig in."

Mirra and Della stood and eagerly began rifling through the clothing racks, leaving Spin to turn the platinum chip over in her hand. It was the most valued currency in the galaxy, and she had enough to buy a lightly armed ship that could take a small crew on her own. That wasn't something she could do legitimately though, she was registered as a slave, so she couldn't purchase anything legally. As an alternative, she could try to run carrying thousands in raw currency on her back. No. If she managed to rescue her friends, she would figure out her next move.

Either the medication wasn't working, or her desire to raid and pillage the Countess' business interests wasn't just a part of her desire for revenge, it was the best option she had. She looked to the pair of women who were enjoying their taste of freedom. Mirra was putting a short, white miniskirt on over her thin green consuit. She looked up at her, smiling, it may have been the best time she'd had in years. Spin nodded and smiled back. "That works for you," she said.

"There's a top, too," Della said, putting a loose fitting tank top on her friend.

Spin didn't have a problem risking her life saving her friends, but she didn't know if she could live with herself if she led those two into a situation where they lost theirs. She caught her reflection in the platinum rectangle in her hand

and saw as much of Larken in her appearance as her own. "Did you find any hair colour stuff?" she asked.

Mirra pulled a tiny box from a small storage crate and handed it to her. "I think I found what I'm wearing," she said, pulling the tank top into place over her consuit. The white skirt and tank top looked right overtop of the green suit, partially because it looked more painted on than worn. The new layer to the outfit offered enough modesty to suit Mirra, it seemed.

Spin held the tiny box up in front of Mirra and clicked a button on the back. "I hope you don't mind if I steal your hair colour."

"No problem, it's the style of the week, now that I can change it whenever I want, anyway."

Spin held the device over her head and it released what seemed like an oil at first, but as she spread it through her hair, it disappeared. The warm brown she ended up with was exactly what she wanted.

"That's nice on you," Della said, taking a few steps in her direction with four different outfits in her hands.

"Thanks," said. "Having trouble choosing?"

"There's so much here," Della said with a hint of despair. "This isn't even all the clothes; this is just what's sellable now."

Mirra and Della helped her try things on for the next two hours. A process that was fun most of the time, a good distraction. As Della found a long, stretchy dress that would go well over a flesh coloured consuit that she took

106

half an hour choosing, Mirra noticed that Spin had gone quiet.

"Are you okay?" she asked her quietly as Della picked and pulled at the dress, making final adjustments to the fit.

"I think I'm ready to move Larken," said.

"Okay," Mirra said.

Spin crossed the cargo bay and took an emergency stretcher down, then Mirra followed her to the cockpit. They gently moved him from there to the small medbay, where they laid him inside an emergency stasis capsule with wheels and closed it. She stood there, with her hands on the foot of the capsule for a long moment, feeling grief that she knew would have her wailing if she wasn't medicated, wash over here.

"Is it okay if I say something for him?" Mirra asked quietly.

Spin nodded.

"Hello, Larken," she said. "I saw you and Spin last night, and you were beautiful together. I know she'll remember you for the rest of her life, and all the good moments you shared together. She's resting her heart now, because she has work to do, but I know she grieves." A tear slipped from Mirra's eye. "She loved you, and she'll remember you. It's good to be known by great people when you pass, and Aspen is a great woman. She set me free today, so I'll watch her for you. I can't take your place, no one can, but I promise to stay with her until I'm sure she doesn't need me, then I'll probably stay a lot longer. We wish you were here, but you've gone on ahead, so be at peace as you roam, and we'll see you again some day."

"Thank you," said, sighing through a wave of grief.

Mirra moved to her side and put her arm around her. "I've seen people cry on that sort of medication before," she wiped a tear from her own eye. "It's okay, we understand."

"Dolls can't cry," she replied. "And call me Spin."

08

Even though they'd done everything they could to help her, Spin was wary of her new friends. She waited until they went to sleep before thinking of where and how she'd rest. They didn't seem to have any misgivings about closing their eyes for a while, taking two of the finest rooms.

Spin decided to look around the cargo bay for survival equipment and she found a sleeping bag before long. The compromise was simple, even though it would definitely show that she still didn't entirely trust her new friends. She would sleep on the floor at the back of the cockpit and lock the door.

Someone, most likely Della, had cleaned the blood and swept up the metal shards from the rounds that killed Larken. You would never know that he died there, even the smell was gone. Spin laid her sleeping bag down on top of where Larken's body was, locked the door, set her alarm, undressed and slipped inside.

Even though her head was spinning as she went over and over the events of the previous day in her head, she found herself dozing off. "Too much happened today," Spin whispered to herself before she finally drifted into a black sleep.

Spin's alarm woke her up by sending gentle, tickling impulses through the computer bonded to her forearm. It felt as though she'd slept for days, and she unlocked the cockpit door, then sat in the pilot's seat.

They were just about to come out of faster than light mode, and the end of the wormhole ahead read all clear. Spin got the navigational computer started on calculating the next jump then stretched and yawned.

The door behind her opened and she yanked her hands back down to cover her chest when she realized that she may have approached her morning tasks in the wrong order. "Get dressed, then check the autopilot," she said to herself.

"What's that?" Della asked as she brought a small cardboard tray and a steaming drink in.

"Nothing, just a note to self," Spin replied. "Can you pass me the suit?"

Della smiled at Spin's strategically placed arms. "I've seen everything already. I'd think you would be more comfortable in your own skin by now."

"I am, I think I just got used to being around spacers. They always wear a consuit underneath their clothes unless they're on a planet or partying, so even when they don't have anything on, they still have a full bodysuit."

"Wow, were you on a small ship?" Della asked, handing her the blue containment suit.

She was dressed in just a few seconds, happy that the inside of the suit was self-cleaning. "I love these things.

Wardrobe choices are simple, getting dressed takes a few seconds, and if you spend enough time in the right one, you forget it's there."

"How long did it take you to get used to a consuit?"

"I never did, not really, not with the crappy ones I could afford. This one's different though, it's worth about a year and a half's pay."

"What? That's insane," Della replied, handing her a non-spill mug. "How big was the ship you served on?"

Spin relaxed and sniffed at the drink, her nostrils filling with the comforting scent of coffee. She pushed the button on the side so the cup stirred in one helping of sweetener and took a sip. "It's been months since I've had real coffee," she said. "Anyway, yeah, it wasn't a large ship, I guess. About the same size as this, but more of it was dedicated to cargo and work. There was a lot less room to relax, and some of the spots on the hull weren't quite as trustworthy as others, so we kept our suits on, even used Hygiene Grubs to get clean sometimes."

"Oh, yuk, the ones that eat dead skin and dirt?"

"Yup, just drop a couple down the front," Spin said, pretending that she was dropping something on her collarbone, "Then two down the back and an hour or two later you pull a fat, happy grub out of your boot."

"Sorry, ew. I always thought spacers were cleaner than grounders," Della said, popping a fold out tray on the outside of the pilot's seat arm up.

"Oh, you should smell the crew after we've been in FTL for a week or two on the Cool Angel. There are some things sponge baths and grubs can't clean, and there was always rationing while we were in high speed transit."

"Rationing, smelly crewmates, and soft patches in the hull," Della said. "I'd have never thought."

"It's a living," Spin said. "We always believed we were working our way up to bigger scores, and that we'd see improvements on the ship, and that helped, but the people you spend your time with are more important. It never got too bad as long as I liked who I was around, and I was free."

"We're going to get some of those people now, right?"

"In a few hours," Spin said, finally deciding that it was time to trust her and Mirra with the details of her plan, to see if they could fit into it.

"I can't wait to meet them," she said. "And I can't wait for them to see you, too. Unless you dressed the same way when you were with them."

Spin scoffed, "nope! When I begged to join their crew they found me programming ground tracking systems in Acosta Docks. I was pretty much in rags, crawling around access tunnels to get to upload the tracking software I made to all their nodes. The dock master wouldn't pay me until it was done, because he didn't believe the ground tracking system could work without an artificial intelligence so I was on scraps."

"Wow, how'd you get there?"

"That's where I landed after getting on an escape shuttle with a bunch of people in Purdue, a city close to the palace I grew up in. Everything I had was stolen the first night, so I arrived in Acosta with nothing. I was there for months, hoping no one would realize I was a doll and deliver me to the Countess. I learned that, when you're dirty, no one looks at you twice, especially if everyone around you is filthy too."

"Good lesson," Della said. "I'd still rather not have to use that one though."

"I don't want to return to that either. Anyway, Sun saw me running across a landing platform, then watched me disappear into a crawlspace with a bunch of old computer equipment, so she kept her eye out and made sure she met me. It took her a few hours, but she found me and asked me what I was doing. I showed her, and she offered me a spot as her second, her Junior Lieutenant, since she just made Lieutenant and had money to pay one."

"So you didn't have to beg," Della said.

"Oh, I had to beg the Captain," Spin said, remembering the convincing and pleading. "I think he agreed because I wouldn't stop, and Sun only encouraged me by blocking the door so he couldn't leave."

"What did you do?" Della asked.

"A lot of what you and Mirra have done for me over the last couple days, taking care of her, the few clothes she had, keeping our quarters tidy, making sure she had what she needed to do her job. When I wasn't doing that I did programming, learned to shoot, taught her martial arts, set up banking and data security. A lot of things she didn't really know how to do as well."

They emerged from faster than light travel, and the communications console blinked. It wasn't something from the Countess' people, the receiving number she set up in the computer wasn't known to them, it could have only been one or two things. Her friends, or her money. Spin held her breath and checked the message.

A stern looking woman with dark hair and a long, pointed blue hat appeared on the screen. "We have transferred the requested amount to your accounts and scrubbed the account number from our systems as an extra measure so you are not captured before you can hold up your end of the bargain. Please send the coordinates for the location of Dexter and Tilly Rinnel as soon as possible. Upon finding them in good condition, we will not pursue legal or direct action. If we find them in poor condition, or if you kidnap a member of our household again, you will suffer." The message ended.

Spin checked the account the money was meant to go in and found 154,000,045 United Core Authority credits. She immediately entered a programming script that sent it on it's way through dozens of accounts that would convert it to strange, alien currencies, put it behind several walls of secrecy upheld by governments large and small, then land it in her real personal account. The number of credits was updated to 43, and she knew it was on its way. A final keystroke sent a message with the coordinates to the Rinnel family representatives. She activated a final macro and changed the contact numbers for the Fleet Feather again. Covering her tracks took work, but she was fairly confident that she'd get what she needed in the end, and no one would be able to successfully trace the messages or money.

"Did I just see what I thought I saw?" Della asked.

Spin activated the FTL system and the ship began slipping into the jump that would take them to her friends on Tullast. She smiled at Della and nodded.

"They actually paid, and fast. It'll take another couple days for the money to make it through all the places I sent it to, and that one-hundred-fifty-four million will look more like a hundred twenty-six when it gets there, but I'll still give you guys your million each, and I'll have more than enough clear money to do whatever I decide."

"Why will it cost so much?" Della asked.

"Every bank I'm sending it through will take a fee, and a few of them take a big bite because they defend their transaction data from everyone. If I didn't do it that way, the Rinnel company could just take it back, telling whatever banks I use that the cash was ill-gotten. I've done it before for the Countess and the Captain of the Cool Angel, it works."

"I didn't realize you kidnapped Tilly and Dexter because you knew how, I thought it was just a spur of the moment thing," Mirra said as she came up the steps.

Spin got out of the pilot's seat and sat down on her sleeping bag so she could pull her boots on. "The Cool Angel's crew stole some things, kidnapped two people, and committed a few other big crimes while I was there. Before I came along they demanded to be paid in cash. After I showed them what I could do, that changed. I still didn't teach them what I knew though, not even Sun."

"So you stayed important to them," Mirra said, handing Spin the bun Della brought for her.

"That's what you do on a crooked mercenary crew," Spin said. "I don't know if I want to be a part of that anymore though, it always felt like desperate times, and even I was looking over my shoulder, and not just for the Countess' people. Still, it's easier to get away with things now that artificial intelligences don't watch every little thing. Programs do, but they can be tricked."

"Speaking of watching," Mirra said. "We wanted you to know, we understand why you played it safe last night."

"Thanks," Spin replied, unsure of what to say. She inspected the warm bun Mirra handed her. "Once you get paid I won't be as worried, because having the money will make you both accomplices."

"You're too good at crime for where you came from," Della said, stopping and turning to Spin apologetically. "I didn't mean to remind you of the Countess and all that, sorry!"

"Don't worry, I know who bought me, where I was raised. I also know I'm as human as anyone, and that I got a better education than most, a lot of that had to do with learning how to rip people off legally, in the name of my masters. Handling finances, making deals, you know, legal stuff that's a moral crime. I was brainwashed into thinking my place was chosen and Larken and I would be together forever with the Countess. I escaped the first time because I thought he was dead, all that programming started falling apart. I have to get used to people looking at me a certain way when they realize I'm a doll that comes from a rich house, I think the whole crew I'm going after will know now. By the way, what's that? It smells good," she said, looking at the bun.

"It's a baked wrap. Sanna Egg rolled in with vegetables and rice then baked, it's really street food where we grew up, only we use much better ingredients, so not so much anymore."

She took a bite and enjoyed the explosion of rich flavours. It was mild, warm and tasted of fresh greens, light egg and sweet bun. Spin chewed for a while and said; "I want to hire both of you forever, but I don't think I could afford you now that you're free. At least stay and cook if I end up with a ship. This is amazing."

"I love cooking," Mirra said. "Almost never got to though, they had chefs."

"You're hired," Spin said, looking at the wrapped bun.

"I can help in the kitchen?" Della asked. "Maybe keep the ship clean?"

"Yup," Spin said, before taking a big bite. Chewing gave her a moment to think about what had to come next, and by the time she was finished she knew how to approach the topic. "I need your help though, and I have to warn you that it's going to be dangerous. I think you can both handle it, but it could be very rough, so I don't want you to feel obligated."

"Just tell us what you need," Mirra said. Della nodded her agreement.

Tullast had become an ugly place. The cities were still burning in some provinces. At some point in time someone came in ships and blasted the world with conventional and electromagnetic pulse bombs, they probably even dropped seekers – unintelligent machines that roved around looking for objects hardened against EMP.

She'd seem one once, covered in drills and cutting tools, made to self destruct as a last resort. Spin could see how dangerous those might be to an artificial intelligence carrying robot who survived an electromagnetic pulse. They were cheaply made, but they could break such a robot apart in seconds and wipe its program out forever.

Regardless of the methods, something had gone and wiped out enough technology in the cities so that the night side of Tullast was almost completely dark. A few massive fires and a couple tiny energy shield domes dotted the land.

It made her nervous, but she flew as low as she could with the transponder and her running lights off. The engines were running at minimum power, even the shields were off just to reduce the ship's energy profile. If they were detected, it would be because someone was looking at exactly the right place with a scanner.

Della was shocked when Spin told her that she needed her to operate a gun turret. She didn't protest more than once, and seemed relieved when Spin explained that her job was to create mayhem and to instil fear, not to actually hit anyone. Spin knew there was a chance that Della could hit one of the people she was there to rescue, so she specifically told the jittery young woman to avoid hitting anyone, just aim for the water around the ship.

Mirra was far less surprised. Apparently she'd spent parts of her childhood in a simulation called 'Interstellar Soldier' for fun. Spin gave her the job of covering the port side, and when the friendly people on the ground were marked, she was to start shooting the slavers. Even if she missed most of the time – real shooting and simulations were two different things – the shooting should drive them under cover.

Spin was to take care of everything else, and she saw herself as a passable pilot, she didn't have the hours of practice it took to build her confidence, but she didn't have much of a choice. The long ship left the cover of the dark cities and skimmed the tops of the trees on the outskirts. The fungus yards were next.

"You can do this, Spin," she said to herself. "You have to do this. No one else is going to take care of your people."

The fungus yards came into view and she slowed down so the ship was hovering on its suspensor field silently then reduced her altitude to a hundred metres. Passive, electronically silent scanners picked up several groups of people. Judging from the way they were moving and where they were, she guessed that her people were in one of two groups. One was a group of four, the other was a group of eight.

"Don't fire yet," Spin said. "And don't hit this red section of the engagement map, I repeat, do not shoot here." She said, marking distillation tanks at the far end of the field. If they were full, they would destroy the terrain and anything on it for a kilometre in all directions, but that was just a guess.

The distillation tower tanks did provide a potential solution. If she could panic the slavers and the guards, they may scatter, leaving the slaves in the pits. Spin pointed the nose of the ship directly at them. She took a deep breath, hoping that they had threat detection on the ground and then set the missiles to target the towers.

Alarms went off in the base right away, it was time to act quickly. With the flipping of a few switches, she turned the scanner suite all the way up, so she could get a reading on the group of four below. The faces, vital statistics and DNA profiles of all four of them appeared and her heart sank, none of them were her people.

A loud ping against the hull reminded her of a step she was missing. "Start firing," Spin said over the intercom. "Remember, do not shoot the highlighted area."

"Gotcha, I see a guard tower, I'm taking it out," Mirra said.

"Making a mess," Della said, giggling as her turret began spewing bolts of fire between the main building and the swampy fungus yard where the water flowed shallowly over foot paths. Spin turned the ship's flood lights on, illuminating the beige, brown and green patches of thick fungus floating atop the hip-deep water.

The four people she scanned waved their hands, flicking water off their soaked sleeves. They were slaves, just like the people she'd come to rescue, so without a second thought she tried to lower the ship so they could get aboard, almost failing. Instead of gently moving down, the ship dropped, dipping into the shallow water then coming up to hover only centimetres above the surface.

Spin focused the scanners on the next group of slaves, there were less than thirty, fewer than expected, and took a few seconds to leave the pilot's seat and activate the control for the port side ramp. The internal sensors reported four aboard in an astonishingly short amount of time. At a glance Spin verified that they would be locked inside the main passenger cabin so they wouldn't wander around the ship.

Spin dropped into the pilot's seat and grinned as the scanners reported five matches with her search criteria. Sun, Boro, Travis, Nigel and Prue were all slogging through the swamp water as fast as they could towards the ship, but they were still hundreds of metres away. She turned the Fleet Feather so the ramp would be facing them, then carefully moved it in their direction.

Seeing that they were about to lose several of their slaves, the guards stopped firing ineffectively on the ship, and trained their rifles on the slaves instead. Spin watched on one of the monitor screens as Boro helped Sun up the ramp, practically shoving her, and was shot several times.

Prue was caught in the line of fire as well, along with two slaves Spin didn't know. The scanners reported that all of them were dead with no chance of recovery, the guards knew how to kill their own.

Everyone who survived made it aboard, and the guards were slaughtering everyone Spin couldn't get to. Della and Mirra were firing as much as the guns would allow them to, in the atmosphere the barrels had to shut down for a few seconds at a time to keep from overheating. "Kill all the guards," Spin said. "They're going to pay for this."

"I'm trying, they're dug in behind cover," Mirra said.

"I have been too," Della said, hitting so seldomly that it looked like she was trying to miss as instructed. Considering she shot at several slaves by mistake – and missed, thankfully – that was partly a blessing.

The hatch reported closed, and Spin raised the ship, backing off to a safe distance as both her missile launchers reported a lock on the distillation towers. They were struck hard on the aft and starboard sides several times, and red lights indicating breaches flashed on a diagram of the ship.

Spin's missile launch system gave her a long, loud tone, indicating that she had a full lock on the towers, and she fired a missile from each launcher. She watched as the missiles passed between the Fleet Feather and their target. The tank tower exploded, lighting the sky and setting the nearby building on fire. It was impressive, the operation was destroyed, but the field was almost untouched, the tanks must have been nearly empty. She took solace in the fact that the place was effectively shut down, it would take years and millions of credits to get it back up and running. That would be the second time in as many years that the Countess would have to revive the operation – the first being when the planet was nullified by the electromagnetic pulse bombardment. Spin doubted the Countess would bother at all.

There was a knock on the pilot door hatch, and Spin ignored it until the shields were up and ship was speeding away from the planet. A glance at the security screen revealed Sun waiting to be let into the cockpit.

Spin set the autopilot and leapt out of her seat to open the door. Sun greeted her with a wet, grateful embrace. "That was the most amazing, reckless, sloppy rescue I've ever seen. Thank you, Aspen, oh God, thank you."

"You smell terrible," Spin laughed.

"I can't tell, my sense of smell died a few hours after we arrived."

"I'm sorry we lost Boro and Prue," Spin said. "If I waited, planned, did some recon before trying that."

"Then more people may have died in the meantime. That fungus was contaminated by something that made it inedible and dangerous, we were using chemicals to restore it, but it was killing us, Aspen," Sun said. "Most slaves were dropping after three days, some lasted five."

"I'm so sorry, all this is because of me," Spin said. "I shouldn't have joined a crew, I should have stayed on my own."

"Hey," Sun said, turning her chin up. "Then I'd have never met you."

"Hey, Aspen!" Nigel called up the stairs. His grinning face looking up at her was good consolation. "I can't believe you rescued us! Don't sweat the people who didn't make it, you did more than most of us could have. Just wondering, do you have a medbay down here? We've gotta get some serious anti-fungal and restorative stuff in us. Well, on us. Um, okay, in and on us and probably on you too just to be safe."

"One sec," Spin said, returning to the controls. There were no fires in the breached sections, but she couldn't help but be alarmed that half the main hold was wide open. The cash they gathered had been moved to a secure cabin, but most of the other loot was still in the hold. The small infirmary was still intact, and they had enough containment to make it to space, then to faster than light travel. The sensors didn't detect any ships in the area, it was eerily quiet in orbit, so she set the navigational computer to start calculating the jump. "Do you have any safe havens in range?" Spin asked Sun.

Sun looked at the navigational screen and pointed at one glimmering point. "Diori. I still have a few friends there, there's no law, and we might get some real help from my old boss in Quino."

"The crime boss?" Spin asked.

"More of a professional looter, salvager now, but he's got a weakness for ladies, so I think we'll have an easy time. Where did you get this ship, by the way?"

"Go get treatment," Spin said, noticing the scabs on Sun's hands and arms. "Tell Nigel not to use any restorative until your infections clear up, that could make them a lot worse."

"Okay, I still need to hear the story behind this rescue," Sun said.

"Later, make sure everyone gets treated right away," Spin said.

"Yes, Ma'am," Sun said with a smile, closing the cockpit door behind her.

Spin locked it, there were too many people she didn't know or trust aboard. "Ladies, are you all right?" she said through the intercom to Della and Mirra.

"I'm all good here," Mirra said. "Nice work. I don't think the Countess will be too happy when she hears about this."

"I hate to say it, but that was fun," Della said. "My turret caught fire for a moment, I got a little burn, but I'm okay."

"Della, when something like that happens, you tell everyone on comms," Mirra said, the sounds of her unbuckling from her seat and getting out of her turret in the background.

"I put it out with an extinguisher and I'm fine," Della said. Her speech sounded slightly slurred and she was breathing more heavily than normal.

"Della, open the door to your turret," Spin said, trying the control from there and getting nothing but an annoying buzz that said the connection between that button and her door was broken.

"I tried, I couldn't," Della said. "Am I stuck in here?"

09

"No, you're fine," Spin said. The navigational computer reported that they were ready to jump, so she initiated the faster than light drive. The next instant she was through he cockpit door and sliding down the stair rails on only her hands.

Travis was already in front of the turret hatch. "Yeah, need a pry bar for that. A hit a couple frames back twisted the doorframe just enough to jam it shut. No air getting to her either, the exchanger vent is blocked somewhere down the line." He coughed wetly.

Mirra arrived in time to hear his explanation. "I'll go find something."

Nigel emerged from the forward hallway completely naked, rubbing lotion on his scabby body. His legs were even more scabbed and irritated than his arms. "I'm all gooped up with anti-fungal cream and took the pills that should make this go away, there's about ninety doses left, so everyone can get some." He said to the cabin with the slaves quietly watching the emergency unfold. There were ten slaves Spin didn't recognize, most of them sitting in posh passenger seating. A few of them laughed at Nigel, who didn't seem to care that he left his clothes in the medbay at all.

"What? My clothes are saturated with the shit we were in down there. I'm not going to let it eat me up, so get used to this ass. By the way, there were a couple places I couldn't reach."

Sun emerged from the medical bay in a paper gown, rubbing lotion on her arms and shoulders.

"I didn't see those, where'd you get that?" Nigel asked, turning and running back to the medbay.

"Middle shelf, forward bulkhead, look for large," Sun said, shaking her head. "Anyone here critical? Coughing, feeling weak?"

"We were just dropped there today," one of the ten said, he was thin, tall, and had a lost expression on his face. "Maybe some of that cream would help, but I think we're okay."

"We'll get you all cream and a pill once the crisis is over," Spin said.

"Okay, I'm Jorin," he said. "Thank you for saving us. Is there someone stuck in there?"

"Yes," Travis coughed.

"I'm going to find something to pry that open with," Spin said. She pulled the flexible helmet for her suit out from her inside jacket pocket, pulled it on and clipped it to the collar, where it sealed and hardened. "I know there's one in the main cargo, but part of that section is open to space."

"Do you need help?" Sun asked. "If you have another suit, I could…"

"Come with me," Spin said, focused on getting Della out. The sensors were dead in her pod, she couldn't tell how much air was left in her turret, but Della had been quiet for several minutes.

Spin ran to the rear hold, Sun behind her, and pointed to a crew berthing. "There's a bunch of suits in there, I'm going to go ahead and get something to break that hatch open with."

"Okay, I'll hurry up."

Spin opened the door and stepped into the pressurized quarter of the cargo bay. Breach doors had sealed off three quarters of the bay, and Spin knew that they'd lost the clothing, a lot of the trinkets, a few real valuables, and a month's supply of food. That stuff was worth ten times what the cash they'd stowed was if they found a half-interested fence. She didn't let it bother her, instead, closing the door behind her and affixing a safety line to the metal loop beside it.

Without hesitation, she opened one of the breech doors and let the air rush from the room. It pulled on her, sweeping her feet out from under her for a moment, but the loop and her line held, keeping her from rushing out with the air under the emergency door as it rolled up. As soon as she regained her feet she hit the release so she could rush into the damaged section of the cargo bay, where a gyro-equipped automatic pry bar was strapped to the bulkhead.

"Spin, she's not breathing," Mirra said, panicked. "All I could find to get the door open were hanger rods, they're not working."

"She's in the cargo bay, I think she found something there, but it's open to space," Sun replied.

The radiation levels were barely within tolerance, and Spin could see the roiling energy tunnel they were travelling through to get away from Tullast. "There's an auto pry bar here." She said as she reached the end of her safety line, there were two metres between her and the tool she needed. "Can't reach it, I'm going to have to move freely."

"We'll find something else, Spin," Sun said.

"This'll get it done. It'll just take a sec, be right back," she replied, detaching the safety line from her wrist and pushing towards the bulkhead. The energy wall of their transit field shifted and roiled beyond it. If she became separated from the ship she'd be lost, atomized as she passed across the edge of the field and into normal space. The only consolation was that it would be quick.

Spin touched the handle of the pry bar and grabbed onto the edge of a support spar, relieved. The pry bar unclipped and came free. That was the easy part. Looking back towards the door she'd come from, she positioned herself carefully, then pushed off.

Spin had practiced space walking twice. Both times it was in an oxygenated environment, inside a ship, with a suit on – just a little training from Sun – but she'd never been in a vacuum with just a thin suit between her and certain death.

The ship turned a little, a minor course correction, something Spin did not see coming. She was pointed at the other end of the broken cargo bay, with only frame supports and no hull between her and the wormhole wall. "Holy shit!" she said, near panic.

"Spread your legs and arms out!" Sun told her. "Get ready to catch anything you can."

Spin remembered those light hearted training sessions then, and did exactly what she was told, using the pry bar as an extension of one arm. To her relief her shoulder collided with a twisted support, and her right arm wrapped around it.

Never had her life seemed more at risk, with an energy wall filling her view, and a slender piece of metal providing her only refuge. The pry bar was near slipping, so she adjusted her hold and brought it closer. "Okay, Sun," she said, breathing heavily. "Get to the cockpit, the door code is three, three, three, five. Make sure this ship doesn't have any course corrections coming up."

"On my way," Sun said, "Nice save, by the way."

"I'm going to have nightmares for weeks about this," Spin said. "I still have the pry bar, Della, hang on," she said, knowing that there was only a slim chance that the woman could hear her.

"Okay, I'm here," Sun said. "No course corrections coming up for nine minutes."

"Okay, I'm going to try this again."

"Push off slowly, you don't have much to work with," Sun said.

"You're telling me," Spin replied. With more care than before, she positioned herself as best as she could, took a breath and pushed off towards the inner door. She was moving so slowly compared to the first push off, she had time to think. "If I don't make it, use whatever you can to get that door open. The ship doesn't matter, she does."

"Shut up, spread your arms and legs open, and get ready to grab on to anything you touch," Sun said. "Silly woman."

Spin waited as she drifted through the cargo hold, open space all around her, aware that she wasn't going to be safe until she actually had a grip on something.

The line she was tethered to earlier brushed against her chest, and she grabbed it greedily, losing her grip on the pry bar. It started slowly spinning out of reach. Her attempt at catching it only made it spin more.

Without a word, she yanked on the line and bashed against the inner cargo hold hatch hard enough to make her teeth rattle. "No way am I losing this thing," she said as she clipped the end of the line onto her wrist, wrapped it around her arm a few times for good measure and pushed off hard, aiming herself at the pry bar.

Spin collided with it and wrapped her arms around the tool, the line stopped her hard, momentarily jarring her. "Okay, coming back."

"Don't ever do that again," Sun said.

With a tug she started drifting back to the inner door. "Activate the emergency bulkhead," she said.

The thin emergency bulkhead began to unroll from the ceiling, stiffening as it straightened down. As soon as it touched the quarter of the cargo bay that was sealed repressurized and she waited. It seemed to take forever.

The interior hatch door finally unlocked once the pressure in the sealed section of cargo bay was equal to that of the hallway, and Spin burst through, running back towards the main cabin. "Here!" she said, handing the pry bar to Nigel, who had it jammed in and activated in seconds. The gyros built into the long pry bar added force to his efforts as he tried to pry the door open. With a long, ponderous creak, the doorframe began to twist. He jostled the end further in. "Stand back."

With one hard push the hatch burst open. "Get her out," Nigel said.

"She should have been wearing her helmet, but she said it felt claustrophobic with it on," Mirra said as she rushed in and pulled her best friend free of the turret seat. Smoke rolled out with her.

Travis arrived with a small revitalizer and put it over her heart. He sat down beside her hard, overtaken by a coughing fit. Spin took over, activating the circular device, then opening the front of Della's suit wide so it could have access. Tendrils poked through her skin to oxygenate her blood, massage her heart back into a beat with physical, chemical and gentle electrical stimulation.

It took over her circulation as it worked on her heart, and presented a breathing cup to place over Della's mouth. Spin pulled the cup mask only to discover that the line was frayed.

"Old fashioned way it is," Spin said, checking Della's airway, straightening her neck and breathing into her. A positive triple beep sounded from the small unit, indicating that there was a regular heartbeat.

Spin kept breathing into Della, regularly. She lost count of the breaths she gave her. "Della, please," Mirra said, picking up her friend's hand. "I don't want to be free and alone." She kissed it.

The breath was suddenly sucked out of Spin's lungs, and she leaned back, her lips still close to Della's. "Della?" she asked.

"Thank you," she said, coughing and wrapping her arms around Spin. "Oh my God, that was scary." The small life-saving device fell off of Della's bare chest. "I'm topless, aren't I?" she whispered.

"Yup," Spin said, making a shallow attempt at pulling the front of her suit closed, but failing.

"There are a lot of people here," Della said.

"Yup, and they're all impressed," Spin said with a chuckle.

Della laughed, coughed, and let Spin go, re-sealing the top of her jumpsuit. You would have never been able to tell that anything had happened to her. Mirra brought her to her feet and embraced her closely. "Don't do that to me," she said.

"I'm okay," Della said, reassuring her.

Mirra pulled her head back and kissed her soundly, and everyone looked on as Della, surprised at first, reciprocated. Sun stopped half way down the steps leading to the bridge and cocked her head, smiling. Then her expression became serious. "Travis?" she asked, rushing to his side.

He was sitting on the deck, leaning forward, passed out. Spin got down to his level and helped Sun lay him out. "He's barely breathing," she said.

"He fell into the swamp as soon as we got there," Leland said. "Got a whole mouth and lung full of that stuff, I doubled his anti-fungal dose, it should be working."

"Unless it's too late," Spin said, her medical training telling her that it almost certainly was. She picked up the revival device and used the medical scanner inside. Its supplies were depleted, and it couldn't help Travis, not with what he had. "It's grown in his lungs, the fungus is dying, but it's causing clotting in his lungs and his bloodstream."

"Can that save him? What can you do?" Sun asked.

The scanner revealed something Spin did not want to know, and she put it down. "There are many clots in his brain, at least twenty, a lot more near his heart. I'm sorry, he's already gone."

"Oh, man," Nigel said, sitting down beside him and touching his face. "We signed on to the Cool Angel together." He touched his friend's hand, then withdrew, running his hand over his face. He looked at Travis with tears in his eyes, and Spin put an arm around him. "He was just bored, fuck. He wanted adventure, to get out there and see the galaxy." In a gesture that made Spin wish she could weep, Nigel gently touched his friend's cheek. "I'm gonna miss you, man."

"There's nothing?" Sun mouthed silently behind Nigel's back.

Spin slowly shook her head. If she wasn't medicated, she'd be in a blubbering pile beside Nigel, but all those emotions seemed just far enough away for her to keep her composure.

"He was the nicest guy," Sun said, putting her hand on Nigel's shoulder. "Worked hard and put other people first."

One of the slaves approached and took the reviver quietly, reactivating the scanning tool on it. Spin didn't stop him. He cleared his shoulder length, dark hair out of his face and checked the results, shaking his head. "It would have happened to all of us eventually if we stayed in that place, he was done for before he got on this ship," he said quietly. "I'm sorry. I can tell you that he's not feeling any of this though. I'm a Medical Technician."

Travis' chest stopped rising and falling. The device beeped an alert and the Medical Technician turned it off. Nigel sighed, his cheeks covered in tears. "See you in the next life, brother."

Sun was on her feet first. "He wanted a burial in space. Is there somewhere we can put him?"

"The medbay for now," Spin said. "There's a stretcher there."

"We can move him," said a pair of rescued slaves. "If you want help."

Mirra led them to the medbay while Spin moved Nigel to a passenger seat. "Listen, Aspen," he said, clearing his eyes and wiping his face. "Whatever you're doing next, if it has anything to do with bringing pain on the people who did this to us, then I'm in. Those fuckers just killed my best friend and my uncle."

Spin had completely forgotten that Nigel was Boro's nephew. To her, he was a friendly man whose humour was so attractive that she couldn't help but flirt with him, but he was family to Nigel. "I can't captain a ship," Spin said. "But I might be able to get us one."

"What do you mean, you can't captain a ship?" Sun asked, her offended tone surprising. "You got free of the Countess, right?"

Della nodded. "She did, and she stole this ship, and planned your rescue on her own, we weren't much help. Oh, she wants to be called Spin now."

"Then you pulled that action hero shit back there to save her," Sun continued. "And who knows what else you had to do to get through the last couple days. Hell, when I looked at the cockpit console, I couldn't help but notice that you hacked this ship so deep that no one could prove it belonged to anyone else unless they checked the serial numbers under the dash. That's some pro level work, *Spin.*"

"I can't be the captain of a ship because I'm about to be the most wanted woman in the sector, and dolls are prohibited from owning anything," Spin retorted. "The word is about to get out, and soon, everyone will know that I'm not a real human, I just have the same flesh and blood as one. They'll also know that I turned on my master, and nothing is more dangerous to the slave trade than one of the most prized auction pieces going rogue. No, I can't be a captain, and we have to dump this ship fast. What's worse is that we're all registered slaves now. Slave hunters won't just be after me, they'll have all your names on the list. Any port run by the UCA or any of their allies are off limits to us."

Everyone in the room was quietly watching her, even Nigel, who would look ridiculous in his baggy jumpsuit if he weren't beside the body of his best friend. "I can afford a ship if we can find someone who will sell us one without ratting on us. To be honest, it would be better to steal one, so we can pretend there's a legitimate captain aboard until we find someone who isn't wanted, someone with a clear name to put a new ship under. Without that, we're stuck with the black markets, the wasted places, and the lawless systems."

"We've been there before," Sun said. "Some of us even have friends in pirate havens, we just need something to trade."

Spin found herself smiling, really smiling for the first time since Larken was killed. She held up her wrist. "I have a download of the Countess's entire personal and corporate database. Shipping routes, banking information waiting to be cracked, locations of operations, caches, you name it."

"That's a start, a good start," Sun said. "But I was thinking we could go get the Cool Angel, and tear Captain

White apart. He betrayed you and threw crewmembers away for a pile of cash. I can't let him get away with that."

"Definitely," Spin said. "So, you're in?"

"Sure, what's the plan after we kill White?" she asked.

"Um, wait, wait," the Medical Technician said. "Can anyone join in, or is this a private party?" His dark eyes were focused on Spin. "I have nothing, they found me barely surviving, scrounging in the wastes like most of these people and then put me to work whether I liked it or not. I'm a great med-tech with years of experience, and I need onto your crew if you're going after them."

"Me too," said one of the rescued slaves behind him, her green eyes peering through a mask of filth and scabs. "I know I can be useful."

All but three of the rescued slaves volunteered. "I'd like to stay too," Della said.

"Even after that?" Spin said. "This won't get easier."

"I look at these people and think about what my masters do," she said. "I want it to stop, I don't want to see another teenager snatched from the street like I was six years ago, and I think I know where we can hit them."

"So do I, Della," Mirra said, setting the stretcher down beside Travis' body. "We're both with you, Spin."

"You're going to have to follow her," Spin said, pointing at Sun. "She's better at this than I am. I was a glorified cabin girl for her."

"Cabin girls don't save a compartment full of people," one of the slaves said. "But I'll follow her if you tell me that she's your creature, and doing your work."

Spin recognized the voice immediately, but couldn't quite put a name to it. It took her several seconds to see through the dirt and scabs, but then she remembered who he was. Governor Dantor, from New Parisia, one of the richest cities in the Core Worlds. "We met right before the tragedy that led to your first escape, it is good to see you free, Aspen. I was your Countess' captive for over a year while she tried to use me to twist governments to her will. When I stopped cooperating she sent me here, so they could put me in that swamp until I was near death, treat me, then put me back. She's used my own position to disgrace me in the meantime, I'm sure." He pulled his hood aside, revealing deep gouges where flesh had to be removed and scabs that looked worse than anyone's. "You've ended my suffering, treated my wounds and offered free transit to a civilized port. I may be out of government, but I must still have some power, and I'll use it to help you crush her."

"All right," Sun said. "Then we need to get another ship fast. Are you sure you have enough, Aspen – I mean, Spin?"

"I have enough," Spin replied.

"How?"

"Kidnapping. I had a few extra minutes and an opportunity I couldn't pass up."

Della's emphatic nodding almost made the comment seem comical. "Best kidnapping ever," she said.

"Okay, and I have someone we can buy one from, maybe," Sun said.

"I can get you clean registrations, multiple transponder codes, and permits for weapons," Governor Dantor said. "Maybe. They might not be good for more than a couple months."

"So, this becomes clear," Sun said. "We're outlaws and information sellers at best, scavengers and runaways at worst.

"Wait, how do we get out of this? How can we get off this wanted slave list?" asked one of the passengers.

"We get the Countess to release us by buying our own freedom, or by killing her and anyone she willed her property to," Sun said.

"Money doesn't mean anything to her," Spin said. "Killing her is our only option for freedom, it's also the hardest. She has children, and people who would inherit her property. We can hide, try to live our lives in shadows, or we run so far that no hunter will come after us."

"Like to the Sercil Sector?"

"No, outside civilization, where humans haven't been before," Spin replied.

"Hell, no," Nigel said. "We hide until the sector gets calm and outlaws slavery everywhere, or until we see an opening and we kill the Countess at a family reunion. Slag the whole inbred bunch of fuckers."

Spin could barely believe it, but Nigel's idea wasn't terrible, just next to impossible. It did lead her to an idea that rested within the realm of possibility. "We could give this away," she said, pointing at the computer display on her skin and the database of information it held. "Take a cut from anyone who uses this information to hurt her and her companies. We make her companies such open targets that every crime lord, small government, slavery opponent and rival corporation takes a bite out of her. We do it until she either has no power left, or until she releases our slave bonds."

"That's genius," Sun said. "Outlaw thinking."

"But what about the meantime? We need cash for protection, food, ships, what about us? We're runaways, outlaws with a mark on our backs," Nigel said.

"We'll take it," Spin said. "No, let's make sure no one sees us that way. If people have to know about us, see us, deal with us at all, let's make sure everyone knows that we're only one thing: pirates."

* * *

Thank you for reading!

Here are two sample chapters from Book 2 of the Chaos Core Series: Cool Pursuit, coming in 2016!

01

The weapon had become an artefact. Objectively, it was a nice gun, with well-polished metal surfaces, a brute spinning calendar inside another atop a trigger and handle. The clip carried only fourteen rounds. It should seem like just another object in the bottom of Spin's bag, but it was the weapon that murdered Larken.

A few of those engineered frack rounds spun from its barrel, broke apart and put great big holes in his torso. She could have put him in stasis with medication if another one hadn't ricocheted and torn through the back of his head. That should have been the end, but he was just conscious enough to look her in the eye, tell her how much he loved her, that she should move on, and then he died in unimaginable agony, squeezing her hand and grinding his teeth together so hard that she could hear the squeak of the enamel.

That weapon reminded her of his last moments. When she thought of him, tried to reach those happy memories, those blood soaked minutes got in the way. She could only see him suffering. The weapon was an artefact, it had become something special, unique. No other thing in the universe had done what that had done.

"Retiring the shredder?" asked Sun as she leaned into the doorway of the quarters Aspen had borrowed for their two-day journey.

"Just saving it for a special occasion," Spin replied. "I found a multiplier pistol in the arms locker. There wasn't much else in there, a few stunners, a bandolier of EMP grenades and a dermal printer."

"High res or?"

"High resolution enough to print new dermal computers, communication links, and whatever else. I already printed a comlink on my jaw. Can you see it?" Aspen asked.

Sun took a look at where Spin pointed at her right jawline. "I can't see it at all, it blended right in."

"I doubt all but the best scanners could pick it up. We'd better keep the printer away from Nigel, or he'll burn it out adding display surfaces to his skin."

"Good thinking, he's already got two comlinks printed somewhere on his face, and both his forearms are stitched up with intelligent displays, so he doesn't need any more upgrades."

"He got the other arm done?" Spin asked.

"Yeah, and most of his back."

"I never understood the need to get a display surface printed into your back. You're the only one who can't see it."

"Ah, he's just a modder junkie, like those people with tattoos in old holos and period flicks."

"I guess so," Spin said. "We're almost in the Diori System?"

"Yeah, a few minutes from emergence," Sun replied. "I've been meaning to ask, are you okay? I heard who Larken was to you, Della told me about it last night. You never talked about him."

"I thought I did. I thought I told you about him. Doesn't matter, when I was on the Cool Angel, I was sure he was dead," Spin said. "I took over a year to move on, and even then I thought about him every day. Less, you know how it is, but still, every day."

"I don't really know how it is, he was like your other half, wasn't he?" Sun asked. "You've also been off on your own a lot, and sleeping half the day."

"I took something, it's taken care of, at least for another three weeks. The sleeping, well, I've mostly been thinking, dreaming." More like brooding, preparing, Spin thought. "Running a lot of katas, doing a lot of yoga to clear my head."

"You don't have to do it alone," Sun said. "And you shouldn't take more of that stuff. Those drugs are for the worst cases, catatonia, constant panic attacks, hypervigilance and delusions."

"When I took that little pill my mind had stopped. I hated everything around me so much that I almost spaced Mirra and Della along with the body of the pilot who killed Larken. Della's tears brought me back to my senses just enough to stop me from doing something horrible, and Mirra calmed me down enough to start thinking a few minutes ahead. If it weren't for this drug, I would be curled up in a ball right in that corner, and I bet you'd still be waist deep in toxic sludge."

"Sounds like you owe more to Dell and Mirra than to any pill."

"Maybe, but I'd rather take a pill every few weeks to dull my grief for Larken and be as useful as I can be for all the time I have left than spend the rest of my life suffering for the loss." Spin closed her duffel bag and walked past her into the corridor. "I'll be fine. Oh, and if you want to practice anything, just ask. I'm sure the whole crew could use it to clear their heads." She continued on to the stairs leading up to the cockpit where Nigel watched the scanners.

"That's not the point, everyone wants to support you while you get through this."

Spin turned and faced Sun at the top of the stairs. "I'm fine. I can't see what anyone could do to help. The meds take the edge off, I can focus on what's important. When I'm not busy with that, I can mope and feel sorry for myself in private."

"Um, coming out of FTL in a few seconds here," Nigel said, getting out of the pilot's seat. "I'll fly this thing if you want, but I'm no pilot."

"No worries, we were finished," Spin said as she dropped into the chair. "I'll take the controls, Sun's distracted by my lack of wailing and whining."

"I think I'll go see if our passengers are ready to go," Nigel said, hastily escaping from the cockpit.

"I'm just watching out for you," Sun said. "If you say you're all right, then okay, but if you need someone to help you through this, I'm here."

"Okay, got it," Spin said. The Fleet Feather emerged from the wormhole and new sensor information was added to the preemptive scans that were already under way. Their destination, Genna Station, was only minutes away. "It's an old colony ship," Spin said. "Shouldn't we be picking up energy readings at this distance though? Maybe some port traffic?"

"Yeah, Genna's always busy," Sun said, adjusting the scanners. "There are usually hundreds of ships around. There's usually an old British Alliance carrier around too, it's the main defence."

Spin increased the range of their scans as she and Sun watched the results come in. There was some wreckage spread across thousands of kilometres, but no active ships or buoys.

"This isn't bad, it's whoa-crazy bad," Nigel called up from below. "I'm watching the scanners, and I'm only picking up basic life support on the station. There are no ships around it, a holy-fuck-ton of damage to the port side, and a few cargo containers tucked in to an open section."

"Is that a metric holy-fuck-ton, or an Issyrian standard measure holy-fuck-ton?" Sun asked as she scanned through the data.

"Either way, I don't think your boy Quino or his people are here. If they are, they must have gotten slagged along with whoever was unlucky enough to see this go down first hand," Nigel said.

"The scrambling field is still up," Sun said. "Just enough signal noise to make small life signs inside impossible to pinpoint. There could be scavengers aboard, we wouldn't be able to see unless there were thirty, maybe forty of them in a small area."

"I'm sure there are," Spin said. "If those containers weren't sign enough, there are still computers in there," Spin said. "Navigational guidance computers, small ones. Our antenna's picking a few of them up, so the cherry pickers and bigger outfits probably haven't found this place yet."

"Excuse me," asked a female voice from below. "We aren't going there, are we? From what I'm overhearing, it sounds bad."

It was one of their less useful passengers, a young woman who was sent to the work camp by the Countess as a punishment. Spin hadn't taken the time to get to know most of them, especially since they were only waiting, eating their food and breathing their air until they reached a somewhat civilized port. "Della," Spin said into her comm.

"Wow, your new communicator's nice and clear. Yes, Spin?"

"Can you make sure our passengers are comfortable?"

"Miss? Are we going there? It sounds dangerous?" the woman at the bottom of the stairs pressed.

Della was there a few seconds later. "Don't worry, they know what they're doing. Just have a seat and we'll tell you what we're doing once we know for sure, okay?"

"I'm just," the woman stammered. "I have to contact my brother, you know, he'll want to know what the Countess did to me. He'll need to know where I am so he can come for me."

"I know. We'll get to civilization soon."

Sun shook her head and leaned away from the scanner displays. "There's maybe a handful of people in there, the scramblers keep me from finding out where, but we won't be alone if we go aboard."

"This may be worth checking though," Spin said. "If I can get one or two of those navigational nodes, the small ones, I could use them to make new hardware transponders. Maybe even add a security layer to our next ship."

"That could save us hundreds of thousands of credits," Sun said. "But I don't want to take too much of a risk. I'm thinking we should move on, leave the vultures to pick at this."

"We just get aboard quick, run for the nearest node, pull one, maybe two of the smallest computers, and run back." The converted colony ship came into view. It was over three kilometres long and two wide with nearly three hundred decks. "We'll do a close pass with the Fleet Feather, try to get past their scramblers and then dock where we don't see scavengers. If this was an official claim..."

"There would be a buoy announcing it," Sun said. "So they're not supposed to be here either."

"Right. So, we might need the tech if we want to make our next ship untraceable, are we getting it?"

Sun thought for a moment, looking at the large grey and green station that filled the cockpit window. "We split up, give ourselves half an hour and bug out."

"An hour, I know we can get some serious tech in one hour. The more we bring to the table when we meet someone who we can trade this ship in to, the better."

"All right, an hour," Sun said. "No risks, if any of us run into armed opposition, we get back here and move on. We'll have to land somewhere in the Diori system to drop our passengers off and ask about Quino, see if his people got off the station."

"Sounds good to me," Spin said, leaving the pilot's seat. "You're the better pilot."

"We'll have to do something about that," Sun said, sitting down. "You need more practice."

"I'll get it."

02

It was like a race, with Nigel, Sun and her all running through the corridors on the starboard side of the station. They stayed away from the control centre and engineering, that is where they'd find serious scavengers. They all took different corridors so they could get as much as possible then get out. "I got one!" Sun said over their encrypted channel.

"What? It's only been five minutes!" Nigel replied. "I'm going deeper, going to find a real jackpot, I bet there's even a store in this section."

"Just get the navigational nodes, they'll be worth a lot more than anything you find in a store," Spin said as she skidded to a stop in front of a panel. There was a node right behind it, cheerily announcing the location, spin rate, trajectory, and other essential data to any systems that would listen. A station that size needed that kind of technology to keep itself together, and to make managing it much easier for the administration. Why they used such high quality components for a simple task was beyond Spin, but from the looks of the darkened corridors, everything in the converted colony ship was top of the line. As she pried the access panel loose and started detaching the palm sized, sealed computer from its interface cables, she wished that she'd had a chance to see the station in its prime. "Got one," she said as the last cable came loose. The computer kept running for several seconds before it powered down. "This one's in an impact case, like a black box."

"Mine was too, whoever had this ship built spent more money than all of us have ever seen put together," Sun said. "This place is going to be crawling with vultures like us in no time."

"Going down a few levels, may be out of comm range for a few minutes, see you back on the ship," Nigel said.

"Don't go too far, Nigel, these aren't worth getting left behind for," Sun said. "Nigel? God dammit, he's already out of range."

"Ooh, my node had a backup," Spin said as she pried a second one loose and disconnected it.

Navigational nodes, or complex micro-quantum computers of the class that were scattered across Genna Station were becoming more difficult to find all the time. No human could effectively ensure that one was made properly on the assembly line, it took complex computing to make them, the kind of computing that artificial intelligences were responsible for before they went rogue. Sure, humans would eventually develop software that could do the same job, but that could take decades.

There was a CMQC at the heart of every ship that served as a genuine, unique transponder, and as long as Spin had the hardware, she could program a convincing fake. If she could bribe an official to enter a fake transponder built with one of those, it would become as good as real, with records backing it up. The thought of having a ship with more than one transponder so they could hide in plain sight made her want to make the hour she had to loot as many of the Genna Station's navigational nodes as possible. If they could get more than three, they could easily wipe out the data on them and sell the hardware as high-end blanks.

"Running to the next one," Spin said as she sprinted down the hallway. Genna Station's gravity, air recyclers and heaters were all still running, and she couldn't figure out why. On a whim, she linked the computer printed on her arm to the next service panel through her suit. "Um, Sun? The station says that emergency self-repair systems are running. That's why life support is back up." She opened her headgear and let it slide into the pocket between her shoulders. "The air even smells clean."

"That's nice, did you get the next node? We don't have time for sightseeing."

"Okay fine, grabbing this node and moving on," Spin said. "I almost feel bad though, it's not like the station will miss a couple dozen of these, there are hundreds throughout, but if a few more scavengers go after the nodes, there could be trouble."

"The next crime lord who takes this place can worry about that. It's not like this place was home to the finest people in the galaxy," Sun said.

"You have a point," Spin said as she dropped another pair of nodes into her hip pocket. "That's four for me."

"I have five, we might just call it quits soon and retreat while the getting's good. We're already ahead of what we thought we'd get."

"And that's not including whatever Nigel is into right now." Spin ran down the hallway, chasing a bright blip on her scanner that told her that the next node, or pair of nodes were several hundred metres down the long corridor. "Still, I'd rather make use of the whole hour, who knows how much we'll find if we risk just a little." The sounds of her thigh-high boot's heels clacking against the deck rang in her ears. The longer she used the things, the more she hated them. Finding some sensible boots was starting to become a priority.

She slowed to a walk for a few moments to catch her breath, admiring the thick transparent metal hull to her left. The view of the stars with little light to interfere was stunning. The brightest part of the galaxy shone before her eyes, a luminescent cloud of stars. For the first time, thinking of Larken, and how she wished he could be seeing that with her didn't only sadden her. She knew him well enough to imagine an expression of wonder. Out of the two of them, he was the one inspired by visual things, and this would have sent his imagination on a wonderful tangent. "I'll see the sights for both of us."

"What's that, Aspen?" Sun asked.

"Nothing, just took a minute to catch my breath," Spin replied, turning towards the corridor that would lead her to at least one node. A four way split in the hallway was coming up. Her scanner beeped a warning as she noticed something move in the darkness, and drew her sidearm as her boots failed to get a good grip on the deck. Spin slid to a stop, still on her feet, brandishing her sidearm at a thickly muscled short man carrying a massive rifle. He aimed it at her, his eyes wide with surprise and stopped as he realized that she'd beaten him to it, and already had her weapon pointed at his head. "Don't move," she said, noticing that he had a taller, much bigger friend to his left.

To her right, the shadows seemed to move in the gloom, and someone in a heavy helmet drew her weapon, pointing it at the largest of the group. "This is definitely not where I saw myself ending up today. Standoffs with three strangers are not on my list of favourite things," Spin said, holding her inertial multiplier sidearm – a vicious looking thing with a five-centimetre-wide pulse emitter on the front – as steady as she could. She loved seeing a standoff in entertainment. The tension, the suspense, and at the end of every great standoff, someone always fired, setting the whole thing off. It was her first time being in one for real, and she was quickly gaining an understanding of the real danger, hoping for a very different ending than the one she usually cheered for.

"What? Did you say you're in a standoff, Aspen?" Sun asked through her comm. Spin was very happy her question couldn't be overheard.

"I'm Spin, just passing through," Spin said. "Leaving, in fact, unless someone has something to say about it."

"I might," the short, muscled rifle bearer said. There was something familiar about his voice.

"I'm coming, I have you on my locator," Sun said.

The tallest of them twitched his weapon to the left, so it was aiming at the helmeted comer, who flicked her pistol's aim at him in return. "I am absolutely, positively certain that I do not have a dog in this fight, no grudge with any of you and I don't want what's here enough to lose my head."

"Scavenger?" the rifle bearer said, and from the sound of his voice she finally realized who he was. Lin Shae, an acquaintance of the captain of the Cool Angel.

She didn't answer, but eyed the muzzle of his massive rifle for a moment, her eyes finally adjusting to the scant light. He didn't have any bags with him, neither did his friend, so they weren't here to pick at the bones of the great ship. Did he track her here? Was he moonlighting as a slave hunter?

Her shoulder complained at how long her arm was outstretched holding the inertial multiplier. It was a large weapon for a handgun, but surprisingly light. No, it wasn't the weight of the thing that had her arm aching, it was how long she'd been aiming it at Lin Shae's head.

He had a much more intimidating weapon, a pulse rifle that looked like he'd torn it off the side of some old starfighter. The other two, one who pointed at Lin, the other who pointed at her, she didn't know. One was probably a henchman for Lin, that was the one that pointed at her, he had a blue and green Mohawk and an absent look on his face – she expected him to start drooling any moment. The other, the one who quickly shifted her aim back to Lin, she didn't know, and it didn't seem like Lin knew the woman in the blacked out helmet either. The thing had bars running down the front in a V and from her body armour, Spin guessed it was a woman, but it was hard to tell for sure. It could have been a small man, or a short alien.

"Aspen." Lin said, his forehead creasing in irritation. "Why's a girl like you stealing from a place like this?"

"Why are you here?"

"That's my business," Lin said. "Just unlucky enough for you to catch up with me. Am I wanted dead, or alive?"

Spin's confusion only deepened as she realized that Lin thought she was tracking him.

"This suspense is killing me, why don't we blast it out and see whose armour is better?" asked Lin.

"I have the best armour, question answered," said the dark helmet. It waved its plasma blaster from Lin, to Spin, to the Mohawk, who actually looked a little intimidated for a quarter second, then back to Lin.

"I'm almost there," Sun said through the comlink she had buried in her jawbone. "God, this ship's big."

"I'm just waiting to see who tires out first. You brought the biggest gun, Lin. You might be regretting it now, though. Just wondering, why are you on this drifting heap?"

"Salvage, my wrecking crew is going to latch on to this old heap any second now."

"Nothing on scans," Sun said, out of breath from running down a corridor somewhere else in the old colony ship. Hopefully somewhere close. "If he had help coming, they're really late or they're already so close to the station that their location is being hidden by the jammers."

"You never could bluff, Lin," Spin said.

"When did you get a chance to see me gamble?"

"You don't remember playing Seven Star on the Cool Angel? The officer's game?"

"Oh, now I remember, you were serving drinks and slinging snacks, some kind of petty officer." Lin adjusted his grip on his outrageously large rifle.

"Getting a little hard to hold on there, Lin?" Spin asked with a smirk.

"I've got hours left in me, *hours,* don't worry."

"So, who's the guy with the unfortunate haircut?" she asked.

"My nephew," Lin replied. "Boy will do anything for me."

His nephew smiled broadly, nodding, his eyes not quite focusing right.

"Family's important. You know, if you're just doing salvage, I'll just leave you to your work after we get a few parts for our ship. There's someone else here though, their jammers are keeping me from seeing where they are though."

"My handiwork. I say you just move along," Lin said without hesitation.

"We only want a few nav nodes, won't mean anything to your bottom line." Spin said.

"Okay, fine. Did you just come here for salvage? Most people don't even know this place was abandoned yet."

"Actually we were looking for Quino, this used to be his place, right?"

"Well, yeah, he shared with a couple other outfits, but not for about nine months. He moved on to Wayland Prime, running an even bigger operation there."

"So, you'll put that down if I promise to grab a couple parts and move on?" Spin said.

"Well, yeah," Lin said.

"Then why did you draw on me?"

"You drew on me first, remember?" Lin asked. "Why is that, anyway?"

"You surprised me, besides, don't you hunt slaves as a side business?"

"No, we used to bounty hunt before the 'bots went crazy and cut up their humans. You know, tracking murderers, big ticket thieves, no slaves though. That's shit-heel work, thug bullshit."

"So, we're all right here, and he's your kin," Spin said. "So, who's this helmet whose pointing her weapon at you?"

Lin glanced at her, then back to Spin, his eyes widening. "Fuck."

"Do you remember Marli Owen's daughter, Terry?" a garbled female voice asked from the black helmet.

"Oh, shit, he took a hit out on me for that?"

"No, you idiot, I'm her, I'm Terry. You didn't even leave a note. I've been tracking you for three weeks."

"Didn't recognize you in the combat armour, how ya been?" Lin asked, trying to sound casual.

Spin lowered her sidearm and dropped it into her thigh holster.

"You gave me the grish. It's in stage two."

Spin's jaw dropped. "Oooooh," Sun and Nigel said over their channel, she could practically hear the pair of them cringing. Of all the sexually transmitted diseases to catch, the grish was the worst. It remained dormant in its first stage, spreading to partners with little trace. Stage two resulted in painful internal and external sores that dripped pus. It took months to treat in that stage, and if you didn't catch it in time, it would move on to phase three, the flesh eating phase.

Lin's nephew looked shocked, glancing from Lin to the helmeted woman over and over again.

"Oh my God," Sun said over the communicator. "I almost slept with him last year. Bullet dodged. But, hey, we could make a friend here."

"A friend who will have us cleaning chairs and toilet seats every time he visits," Nigel said. "What did I just start hearing? I just got back into range."

"Never mind, we'll catch you up later," Sun said.

"At least you're not pregnant?" Lin told Terry with a shrug.

The sound of a loose panel somewhere down the dark corridor made everyone flinch. The corridor intersection was flooded with bright light as the helmeted former lover fired. Spin understood what Sun was getting to, they could make an ally – if a sleazy one – out of Lin. Even though Spin thought he deserved what he had coming, at least a little, she leapt at the armoured woman, tackling her to the ground.

To her surprise, the Terry batted her hard enough to knock the wind out of her and send her sliding more than a dozen metres down the hallway. As soon as she started to slow down, Spin rolled into a side corridor, a short range plasma bolt narrowly missing her.

The nephew took the opportunity and opened fire on the helmeted woman, peppering her with blazing energy shots until she was a heap on the floor. "Everything okay, Spin?" Sun asked.

"I got clear, and Terry the dark helmet girl is a hot pile. Don't know about Lin, I'm going to check now," Spin said as she rushed back to the hall intersection.

"Good, I'm one hatch away, but have to cut through."

"I'll be here." Spin was already reaching into her jacket for her emergency patch kit.

"Fuck, that was my good arm," Lin groaned as he laid on his intact side. The stump of his right arm was a burnt mess, and there wasn't enough of the arm left to reattach. "Thanks for slagging that bitch, Jon."

"You kinda had it coming," Spin said as she knelt down with a tension patch. "This is going to hurt like crazy before the medication kicks in." Lin screamed as she stretched it over his stump and it conformed to the end, wrapping the wound up to his shoulder and affixing itself tightly.

Jon, who was carefully prying the helmet off Terry's head, only spared his screaming uncle a short glance.

"Okay, the meds are kicking in," Lin said, panting. "You didn't have anything that you could have given me first?"

"Sure I did, but I thought you deserved some misery for passing the grish around, I mean, seriously, who doesn't use protection these days? It's not like there's a clinic on every corner."

"I lost a fucking arm and you're giving me shit about not sealing up before getting it up?" Lin asked.

Jon laughed, it was a low, breathy sound. "This might fit you," he said as he offered the helmet to Spin.

Spin looked at it and at the woman on the deck. The only thing not reduced to a burnt pile of human remains was her face, which was twisted in an expression of fury and pain. "Thank you, Jon," she said. "I think I'll clean it before trying it on though."

"We'll be going back to the ship," Lin groaned. "Jon, pick up my quad blaster."

Jon did so, then pried Lin's disembodied hand off the handle and offered it to him.

"Don't think there's enough arm to put that back on, buddy," Lin said.

"Wait, you're not going to wait for your scavenging ship? Maybe they could take care of you."

"No, I'll fess up. We're scouting for Kiren Arms. I was just taking a run through the ship here to see if there were any high end trinkets we could grab before we reported this gold mine. I thought we'd have a good payday coming, but it looks like I'll be spending it all on a new arm."

"And some serious anti-fungal treatments," Sun said as she emerged from a side passage. Like Spin, she was in a thick, form-fitted containment suit, only hers was dark red. Her white jacket was armoured, but not quite as well made as Spin's, which was black and had a refractive coating on top that made it seem darkly multi-coloured.

"What? Is the Cool Angel right behind?" Lin said.

"No, we broke away from that crew a while ago," Sun replied. "You've seen better days."

"You're not here because of some unrequited thing, are you? Already had one former sex-type-thing track me down today."

"Absolutely not," Sun said emphatically. "We just bumped into you by luck. We had no idea there was anyone else aboard."

"Speaking of which, there are pickers aboard, I've been avoiding them for hours, and my knees are getting a little wobbly. The meds are doing me a lot of good, so I should get back to the ship. Take whatever you can carry, it'll be two days before we report this thing as abandoned and a salvage crew dig in."

164

"We'll help you to your ship if you or your nephew tell us all about the places a few people who want to avoid the law may do business. We're looking for a safe harbour to operate out of, and someone who will trade with people trying to avoid the law. Someone who won't turn an escaped slave in."

"Sure thing," Lin said. Jon picked his uncle up, a feat that seemed easy even though he was only slightly larger than him. "I'll even set you up with our ident, so you can call us up later. You know, in case you need anything, or want to get together."

"Thanks," Sun said. "But just business."

"Sure, just don't share what happened here, I have a reputation."

"No problem, the more you share, the less we'll share," Spin said.

"Deal."

* * *

www.randolphlalonde.com